"If we're going to appear as if we're a couple, we need to know more than just each other's names."

"Why didn't you come out and ask, if you wanted to know something about me?" McKayla asked.

"All right. Why didn't you ever get married?"

"I don't think the doctor's going to ask that one, Cade. As far as he knows, I *am* married. To you. But for your information, there was never enough time to cultivate romance."

"Sometimes," he said quietly, "it doesn't have to be cultivated—sometimes it just happens."

Something in his tone rippled along McKayla's skin, whispering its way into her pores. It unnerved her. But as he lowered his mouth to hers, she couldn't quite move away. McKayla had always prided herself on her strength of character. But there was something incredibly enticing about being held this way, as if she were something fragile. As if she needed to be cared for.

Dear Reader,

Welcome to another month of fabulous reading from Silhouette Intimate Moments, the line that brings you excitement along with your romance every month. As I'm sure you've already noticed, the month begins with a return to CONARD COUNTY, in *Involuntary Daddy,* by bestselling author Rachel Lee. As always, her hero and heroine will live in your heart long after you've turned the last page, along with an irresistible baby boy nicknamed Peanut. You'll wish you could take him home yourself.

Award winner Marie Ferrarella completes her CHILDFINDERS, INC. trilogy with *Hero in the Nick of Time,* about a fake marriage that's destined to become real, and not one, but *two,* safely recovered children. Marilyn Pappano offers the second installment of her HEARTBREAK CANYON miniseries, *The Horseman's Bride.* This Oklahoma native certainly has a way with a Western man! After too long away, Doreen Owens Malek returns with our MEN IN BLUE title, *An Officer and a Gentle Woman,* about a cop falling in love with his prime suspect. Kylie Brant brings us the third of THE SULLIVAN BROTHERS in *Falling Hard and Fast,* a steamy read that will have your heart racing. Finally, welcome RaeAnne Thayne, whose debut book for the line, *The Wrangler and the Runaway Mom,* is also a WAY OUT WEST title. You'll be happy to know that her second book is already scheduled.

Enjoy them all—and then come back again next month, when once again Silhouette Intimate Moments brings you six of the best and most exciting romances around.

Yours,

Leslie J. Wainger
Executive Senior Editor

Please address questions and book requests to:
Silhouette Reader Service
U.S.: 3010 Walden Ave., P.O. Box 1325, Buffalo, NY 14269
Canadian: P.O. Box 609, Fort Erie, Ont. L2A 5X3

MARIE FERRARELLA

HERO IN THE NICK OF TIME

Silhouette®

INTIMATE MOMENTS®

Published by Silhouette Books

America's Publisher of Contemporary Romance

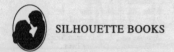 SILHOUETTE BOOKS

ISBN 0-373-07956-7

HERO IN THE NICK OF TIME

Copyright © 1999 by Marie Rydzynski-Ferrarella

All rights reserved. Except for use in any review, the reproduction or utilization of this work in whole or in part in any form by any electronic, mechanical or other means, now known or hereafter invented, including xerography, photocopying and recording, or in any information storage or retrieval system, is forbidden without the written permission of the editorial office, Silhouette Books, 300 East 42nd Street, New York, NY 10017 U.S.A.

All characters in this book have no existence outside the imagination of the author and have no relation whatsoever to anyone bearing the same name or names. They are not even distantly inspired by any individual known or unknown to the author, and all incidents are pure invention.

This edition published by arrangement with Harlequin Books S.A.

® and TM are trademarks of Harlequin Books S.A., used under license. Trademarks indicated with ® are registered in the United States Patent and Trademark Office, the Canadian Trade Marks Office and in other countries.

Visit us at www.romance.net

Printed in U.S.A.

Books by Marie Ferrarella

Books by Marie Ferrarella writing as Marie Nicole

To Charlie,
Rocky's hero.
And mine.

Chapter 1

"Where are you?"

The dark, shining eyes, so like his own, looked back at Cade Townsend. Breaking his heart.

Like a blind man using the tips of his fingers to read the contours of the face of the child before him, Cade moved his fingertips along the face of his son.

But instead of the soft, downy skin and small curves that should have met his touch when it came in contact with the three-year-old's face, his fingers came in contact with a cold, hard surface. The glass in front of Darin's framed four-by-five photograph.

There was no laughter to fill the room, only laughter in his memory, date-stamped three years ago. Three years today.

Today was Darin's birthday.

Today was the day he'd lost Darin.

The memory that was never far away rushed for-

ward, solidifying in vivid colors. He'd taken Darin to
an amusement park to celebrate the occasion. The
kind with rides and noise and music. Darin hadn't
known where to look first. Everything had fascinated
him. Cade smiled fondly at the photograph. Mind like
a sponge, absorbing everything. Retaining everything.
Darin had been his special gift, especially after Elaine
had died.

The day, Cade had insisted, belonged to the two of
them. He'd wanted to celebrate it with his son. Later
in the day there'd be time for the party and gifts.

Later never came.

In the days and weeks following Darin's disap-
pearance from the park, his personal search had
turned into a crusade. Cade's writing career fell by
the wayside. The bottle had called to him, offering
temporary anesthesia and permanent oblivion down
the line. But his father had gone that route, breaking
his neck while in an alcohol-induced stupor and dying
at the age of thirty-two. Cade wasn't about to pass
that sort of legacy on to Darin.

Determined to glean some good out of the soul-
torturing situation for Darin's sake, Cade founded
ChildFinders, Inc. The Southern California-based
agency was dedicated to finding missing children,
whether abductees or runaways, and reuniting them
with their families.

Unique in its purpose, the organization had a stunning track record. It was batting almost a thousand.
Every missing child Cade and his two associates had
been asked to search for had been recovered.

Except for Darin.

Darin, the reason he had begun the agency, the reason he drew breath every morning, was still among the missing.

There were times that Cade felt as if he were tilting at windmills, with despair as his very real opponent. Those times, it was difficult not to believe that his son had vanished off the very face of the earth. Except he couldn't allow himself to believe that. Not if he were to function, not if he were to be any good to anyone. The pain was like a steel bear trap closing around his heart, but little by little, he'd learned to deal with it. To ignore it for long lengths of time. Long enough to be of use to others.

But on days like today, days that carried so much personal significance, when the memories came charging back, attacking him on all sides with a vengeance, it was particularly hard to stay ahead of the pain and not let it just engulf him.

What good would that do? his mind posed.

It wasn't until she cleared her throat that Cade realized he wasn't alone in this office room. There was a woman standing in his doorway. Statuesque, lean, with swirls of deep auburn hair framing her face and edgy agitation leaving its stamp on her. Her demeanor suggested she'd been standing there a minute, perhaps even more, observing him. Giving him his moment, but impatient about the grant.

With the deadly calm that stemmed from his one-quarter Cherokee heritage, the calm he had learned to arm himself with, Cade replaced the framed photograph on his desk where it caught the afternoon light. Only when he was satisfied with its position did he raise his eyes to the dark-haired woman, giving her his attention.

"May I help you?" He half rose in his seat as he asked.

McKayla Dellaventura hadn't wanted to interrupt, but at the same time, she'd wanted to grasp his arm and drag him out of the office, filling him in on the details of the search as they hurried to her car. The words *too late* ricocheted endlessly in her mind.

She nodded toward the hallway. "Your secretary said it was all right to come in."

He raised his brow. "My secretary's out sick."

She didn't like being confused. It wasn't her natural state. Being on top of everything was. That was why the situation she found herself in was doubly difficult for her. She glanced over her shoulder toward the outer office, which was empty now.

"A blond woman…" She trailed off, thinking that should have rung a bell for him.

Now Cade understood. "That would be Megan. My partner. One of my partners," he amended. At times, it was hard keeping track of the fluctuating basic structure of the agency, it was growing so fast. They'd gone from one to two partners almost immediately.

Megan Andreini, the special agent who had been attached to the FBI unit searching for his son, motivated by personal reasons, quit her job with the bureau and joined ChildFinders, Inc. A year into it, they had acquired Sam Walters, an ex-policeman, and just recently, Megan's younger brother, Rusty, fresh out of college with dual degrees in criminology and law enforcement, had joined the agency. There was certainly enough work coming in. The trickle was now a very steady stream, threatening to become a flood.

And each job represented a child who had disappeared.

It made him ill to think about it.

Blocking out the thought, Cade gestured toward the chair in front of his desk. "Won't you have a seat?"

The woman perched more than sat, the hum of nervous energy all but visibly vibrating around her. It was something he had come to expect from the people who entered his agency. He saw them at their worst, and their best. Shattered souls who were trying their hardest to keep up a brave front. Tortured men and women who broke down and sobbed in front of a stranger. Sobbed because their lives had been torn apart.

The woman before him didn't look like a crier, he thought. She looked as if she were ready to run headlong into whoever it was who had taken the child away from her and out of her life.

He'd become a fairly good judge of character, sitting behind this desk. This woman looked every inch the fighter.

"I don't know where to begin."

That, too, he was accustomed to. "Any place you want," he told her softly. "We'll sort it out as you go along." When she still looked undecided, he added, "Telling me your name might help."

Mac felt like an idiot. How could she forget to introduce herself? *Because this situation is like nothing you've ever been in before, that's why,* she thought irritably.

With a toss of her head, she said, "Oh, yes, of course. I'm McKayla Dellaventura. Dr. McKayla Dellaventura," she amended, as if the title that had taken her so long to earn was merely an afterthought. "Dental, not medical," she explained. She realized how disjointed she had to sound, like a videotape that fitfully stopped and started, only to stop again. "I'm sorry, everything is still so jumbled."

Cade knew the feeling was one that faded, but never truly left. It wouldn't until the moment she was reunited with the missing child. But she didn't need to be told that.

"Take your time," he advised.

His voice, deep and rich, had a soothing effect. For just a moment, Mac allowed it to wash over her and take root. Ever since the accident, she felt as if she were running through an emotional minefield, never knowing where the next bomb was and when it might go off.

She slid a little farther down the seat, almost off it entirely. "I'd like you to help me find my niece. She's been kidnapped."

Cade took out a very worn leather-bound notebook from his shirt pocket, turning to a fresh page. He made a notation before looking up. He needed a wealth of details and began to help the woman along in providing them. "You have reason to believe she's been kidnapped."

"Reason?" Mac laughed shortly. "Oh, yes, we have 'reason' to believe she's been kidnapped." Her outrage at the situation got the better of her. What kind of a monster steals a child from the scene of an accident? "She's an eighteen-month-old girl, not quite old enough to drive away on her own yet."

Mac caught herself and blew out a breath. Her brother Danny had always warned her that her mouth would get her in trouble. She flashed Cade an apologetic half smile.

"I'm sorry, that was uncalled-for. I've been given the runaround a lot lately." She dragged polish-free nails through a tangle of deep auburn hair. "My sister was in a car accident two days ago. When the paramedics arrived, one of them said he thought that because of my niece's injuries, Heather might need more specialized care than the hospital in the immediate area could provide. He called a second ambulance to take her to Mission Memorial." Her green eyes darkened. "The only problem was, the ambulance never arrived at the hospital with Heather."

She remembered the raw disbelief that had ricocheted through her when she'd gone down to Mission Memorial to inquire about Heather. Annoyance had turned into cold fear. She remembered, too, the call home to tell her parents that their only grandchild was missing. And she had been the one to tell her sister, Moira, not wanting to leave that to either of her parents. Remembered how helpless she'd felt, standing there, watching Moira as her body had convulsed with sobs.

There was no way any of them were going to continue to endure this agony indefinitely. She was going to find Heather or die in the attempt.

Forcing herself to rein in her own inner turmoil, Mac continued. "As far as everyone knows, the ambulance was stolen or hijacked." She was leaning against the desk now, her eyes holding Cade's. "The upshot is that my niece is out there somewhere, and I want her found as fast as is humanly possible."

There were still more questions than answers here, Cade thought. "Your sister—"

Anticipating his question, Mac jumped in with an answer. "Is lying in a hospital bed in Harris Memorial Hospital right now and, quite frankly, doesn't feel like it's worth living anymore." Two years apart, they were close enough for her to sense that without words. Moira was the delicate one in the family, the shy beauty whose ways could never have been Mac's. But there was boundless love between the sisters, and Mac meant to protect Moira any way she could. "The family's authorized me to act on her behalf."

"The family?" The situation was dire, as always, but the term almost managed to bring a smile to Cade's lips. It sounded like something he might have heard in an old movie about the Mafia.

Impatience clawed at Mac. She'd spent two days spinning her wheels, getting mired deeper in the mud for her trouble. She wanted to be out and about, *doing* something useful. Productive. Finding Heather before something happened to her. That it might already have was something she refused to think about, keeping the thought instead under heavy lock and key, away from the light of day.

"My father, mother, brothers, sister—family," she repeated tersely, her very manner challenging him.

There was no question about it, he was dealing with a type A personality, Cade thought. Since he was, by nature, methodical and even-paced, he felt that some adjustment was necessary. The adjustment would have to be on her part, because he wasn't about to abandon a method that worked for him. "Have you received a note?"

"No."

He jotted that down, underlining the word twice. No note was usually not a good sign. But in this case, there might be extenuating circumstances to consider. He raised his eyes to hers, noting that hers were intensely green now.

"Any reason to suspect that kidnapping was the main intention?"

The soothing element in his voice was beginning to have the reverse effect. Mac curbed the urge to jump to her feet and pull him to his as well. "Heather's gone, isn't that reason enough?"

The woman was obviously intelligent, and it was just her impatience that blinded her to something so obvious as what they might be dealing with. Cade began to explain his reasoning to her, wondering if she was going to feel as if he was being patronizing.

"No, what I mean is that whoever took the ambulance might have taken it for another reason entirely. They might not have even known that your niece was in the ambulance until after they took it."

Mac found the thought chilling. "Is that supposed to comfort me?" She didn't know if that made the situation better or worse and didn't have the time to try to analyze it. Every moment was precious. "Either way, she's still gone."

"You're right," he allowed, "but if the intention was to steal the ambulance and not the child, there's a large chance that whoever stole the ambulance will leave your niece somewhere conspicuous where she can be found and eventually returned."

No, she thought, that still didn't make her feel better. It meant that Heather had been left somewhere to meet possible dire consequences. She couldn't let her mind go there, either. She was beginning to feel like a rat in a maze with all the passages being closed off, one after another.

In mounting desperation, Mac laid her cards on the table. "I don't mean to sound like a broken record, Mr. Townsend, but while you are expounding on theories, my niece is still missing." Pulling herself together, she rattled off the details of the ongoing investigation to the best of her knowledge. "The police are trying to locate the missing ambulance and the paramedics who were in it, but so far, they've had no luck." She saw Cade opening his mouth and anticipated what he was about to say. "I appreciate the fact that they're doing what they can, so spare me that speech, please. But they've got a lot more to keep them busy than just my missing niece. I can't tell them what to do."

Cade had more than a passing hunch that Dr. McKayla Dellaventura had already tried to commandeer the Bedford, California, police department and instruct them on what to do, only to have failed—not for lack of effort on her part, he was sure.

"But you can tell *me* what to do?"

If there was something amusing going on here, Mac didn't notice it. "Paying your fee should entitle me to something."

It took effort to keep from snapping the words at him. Though she had a habit of plowing ahead, she wasn't usually this abrupt with people. But although conscious of her shortcomings here, Mac couldn't be bothered trying to police herself. There was too much at stake.

Cade studied her for a second before speaking. He wasn't annoyed, but he felt that the good doctor had to be made aware of exactly how things operated here.

"It entitles you, Dr. Dellaventura," he informed her in slow, measured cadence, "to my very best efforts in locating your missing niece. It does not entitle you to tell me how to conduct my investigation. That is up to my discretion and the discretion of the people who work at ChildFinders, Inc. In short, you're paying for expertise, not to play leader of the pack." He searched her face to see if the message was sinking in. He couldn't tell. "Any questions?"

She probably had that coming, Mac thought. At least the man wasn't a pushover, or some smooth-talking bureaucrat.

The slightest of smiles quirked her mouth. "Well, at least I don't feel bad anymore about being testy toward you when I first walked in."

He smiled at her. Maybe he had sounded a little harsh, but Cade had a feeling that anything less wouldn't have made a dent. "That wasn't supposed to come out as a lecture."

She shook her head, sending dark waves of hair swirling around her face and shoulders. "Doesn't matter. My feelings don't figure into this mix, Mr. Townsend. All that matters, all that counts, is finding Heather. Alive," she emphasized. She allowed herself a momentary break from form, confessing, "I have this terrible feeling that if we don't find her soon, we never will."

She didn't strike Cade as the type to walk into a situation cold, without knowing the lay of the land.

And it was a known, publicized fact that the more time that passed after an abduction, the less likely successful recovery of the missing child was apt to be. Memories faded, people became confused, forgetful. Facts became jumbled, clues lost or overlooked.

"If we don't find Heather," she continued, trying not to think what that would mean to her and the others, let alone her sister, "Moira won't have the strength to pull through." She was sure of that as well. More than anything, Moira's life seemed to hang by a thread. And that thread was finding Heather.

"Your sister," he guessed.

"My sister," she echoed, nodding as she realized that she'd forgotten to give him Moira's name. Only showed how very rattled this had all left her. "Her full name is Moira McGuire."

He read the look in her eyes and guessed that the sisters were close. And of the two, Mac was probably the caretaker. Either that, or the steamroller.

Mac drew herself up, seeming to grow an inch taller in the chair. "You'll take the case?"

All things considered, it should have been a question. But it was less of a question than a forceful statement. Cade had a feeling that saying no to this woman was never an easy matter.

"All my operatives are busy with cases of their own," he began.

She cut him off. "I didn't ask about them, Mr. Townsend," she told him coolly. "I—my family," she amended, although she had been the one to bring the matter up, as well as being the one who had found the name of the agency to begin with, "would like *you* on it."

Fleetingly, Cade thought of defending his partners, all of whom were excellent, but he had a feeling that anything he said would fall on deaf ears. She had obviously made up her mind. And there was no reason to make her think that he wasn't going to take the case. At the moment, he was the only one in the organization who was free.

Nodding his agreement, he began to explain, "I just wrapped up a case last night—"

"Good, that means you're available."

He wondered if she'd gotten her training in the military and just how difficult it was going to be interfacing with this woman. If he had any sense, he'd pass.

God knew he was pushing the envelope, accepting this. He was drained. Emotionally and physically spent. If he were a pile of coins, he could have been down to the last penny. What he needed was a vacation.

But he couldn't take a vacation from his mind, and that was all that counted. And he certainly couldn't just sit here, staring at Darin's photograph, looking at the calendar and going slowly crazy. He'd be insane inside a week. He wouldn't be any good to anyone then, least of all to Darin when they found him.

Not if, but when.

Cade held on to that slim thread of hope as firmly as he instructed all his clients to hold on to theirs. The difference being, their ships had come in. His was still lost at sea.

Looking at the woman, he held back his answer for

a moment. The smile on his lips peeled back slowly. "I would have pegged you as an only child."

Distracted momentarily by the expression that seemed to change the contours of his proud, angular face, Mac blinked. Where had that observation come from? "Why?"

"You sound accustomed to getting your own way."

Coming from him it sounded less of a criticism than an observation. She let it go as such. "Being an only child has nothing to do with that. The courage of your convictions, my father used to tell me, would see me through. I'm convinced you're the best man for the job and convinced that if there's a way to get Heather back, you're the one who can do it. Do we have a deal?" Mac pressed.

"I'm flattered, Ms.—Dr. Dellaventura."

It hadn't been her intent to flatter him. She was only telling him the truth. She shrugged, her shoulders moving restlessly beneath her blue suit. "If that helps, fine. You'll also be well paid. Over and above your usual fee."

Flares went up, alerting Cade. People did not throw money around for no reason, even people who were well off, as she apparently seemed to be. Of late, a trend had begun to take over at the agency. As of yet, it hadn't overtaken him, but Cade had a hunch that his number was up.

"And why would you be paying me over and above my standard fee, Dr. Dellaventura?"

"The name's Mac," she informed him. "I figure you might as well get used to it since we're going to be living in each other's shadow until Heather's found."

Chapter 2

"Living in each other's shadow," Cade repeated.

When the woman nodded as if what she was proposing was the most plausible of suggestions, he could only shake his head incredulously.

His first rule was to work alone. People tended to get in his way. He was a team player only in the sense that he would return to interact with the team sporadically and at his own discretion.

Sitting back in his chair, Cade studied McKayla before finally saying, "Unless you're paying me to be your backup in a mime performance, I seriously doubt your terminology applies here."

Mac had butted against enough heads to know hard-line opposition when she saw it. She handled it the only way she knew how. She plowed straight through it. "It applies, Mr. Townsend. I intend to work with you on this investigation."

At this point in his career, Cade figured he would probably have trouble working with a trained professional, and she was as far from that as was humanly possible.

He smiled with a touch of indulgence. "My teeth don't need cleaning."

It was a common-enough mistake, given her gender, but Mac didn't feel very forgiving at the moment. "I'm a pediatric dentist, not a hygienist."

Cade had never gotten into the battle of the sexes. To him a person was a person, gender and other distinguishing features were secondary, just so many colorful strokes on comparable canvases.

He inclined his head. "My mistake."

His knowledge, or lack thereof, of her field wasn't important at the moment. Something else was. Rising to her feet, Mac leaned over his desk. "Your mistake, Mr. Townsend, is in thinking that a person can only do one thing and nothing more. I minored in law enforcement."

She didn't add that she was damn good at it, or that she'd briefly flirted with the idea of joining the police force. He'd only think she was trying to impress him. She wasn't. All she was doing was trying to convince Cade Townsend that she wouldn't be a deadweight during his investigation.

The woman didn't give up, Cade would give her that. Tall and willowy, she still reminded him of a Scottish terrier, unwilling to open her mouth once she'd clamped her teeth around something.

"I minored in studio art," he told her. Art had been a fleeting passion for him. It was in his first art class that he'd met Elaine—and fallen in love with a number two pencil in his hand. "That doesn't make me Jackson Pollock."

"No," Mac agreed in an easy tone that belied the agitation within, "that makes you Cade Townsend, someone who might be just as good or better than the aforementioned artist—in your own way," she emphasized. "We're all multilayered, Mr. Townsend, and we shouldn't be afraid to delve into those layers."

The phrase "talk the ears off a brass monkey" floated through Cade's mind. The words fit the woman in his office to a T. "Was that law enforcement or just law that you minored in?"

"Law enforcement," Mac repeated. She couldn't tell if she was wearing him down or not. There was no indication in his eyes, and it frustrated her. She wasn't about to be out-argued. Mac had been at the game all of her life, bucking odds, fighting for every inch she gained. She was very good at holding her own and even better at winning. "You'll be doing my patients a service if you let me come along."

"And how's that?"

"I don't have my mind on my work."

Even though Mac's patients had always come first for her, she'd felt scattered and anxious since the accident. Worried about her sister, about her niece and about the effect all of this was having on her family, particularly her mother, who had always been in poor health. For the first time in her life, Mac was having trouble pulling her mind together and concentrating. The best thing she could do for everyone concerned, herself included, was to find Heather as quickly as possible. Any other course of action had *disaster* and *failure* written all over it.

"The threat of lawsuits should prevent your mind from straying too far."

She was obviously wasting precious time debating with this man. If he had some sort of prejudice about working with women he couldn't overcome, so be it. Mac wasn't looking to make a true believer out of him, she was just trying to get someone who'd be willing to let her work with him.

She glanced toward the door behind her. "Perhaps another one of your operatives might not have as much of an objection to having someone come along on the investigation."

Cade thought of Rusty, who had no set procedures as yet. Rusty would have been the likely candidate, if he wasn't already working on a case. Megan and Sam were both in the middle of cases as well. He'd just checked with them this morning when he'd come in.

That left only him.

"Perhaps not, but they're all busy on other cases." She was still standing over him, as if hovering might help convince him. Studying her, Cade tried to second-guess what was going on in her head. "I'm not sure just what you think is going to happen here, but working a case like this requires a lot of slow piecing together." More likely than not, she was weaned on Hollywood's idea of what a private investigator was and did. "There's very little high-energy racing around, very little 'bursting in with guns drawn' type of thing. It's methodical, painstaking work. More along the lines of putting tiny mosaic tiles together in order to get at a much larger whole." Every speck, every report from the crime scene was a potential clue waiting to be linked up to another to make the all-important whole.

If he was hoping to make her back off with his analogy, he was in for a sad surprise, Mac thought. Her mother had once said her middle name should have been Tenacious instead of Theresa. "I put my first thousand-piece puzzle together at the age of eight."

Amused, Cade whistled softly. Her determination obviously had some very deep roots. "You're just an all-round overachiever, aren't you?"

"I've been called a royal pain at times, Mr. Townsend, but I can also think on my feet. I promise you that I'll be more of a help than a hindrance. You'll be in charge," Mac told him. It was understood that she was giving him her word. "Anything you say goes."

He laughed shortly. "I doubt that. I've already told you no and that doesn't seem to be getting me very far."

"All right," she conceded, "with some reservations." Her eyes became very, very serious. She was pleading with him as much as she was able to plead. "I'm trying to save my niece and my younger sister, Mr. Townsend. Moira lost her husband in a car accident just before Heather was born. Financially, she is well off. Emotionally is another story. She's not as resilient as I am."

Cade caught himself thinking that probably very few women could be.

"Another blow will probably break her. I'm not

about to let that happen," she told him fiercely. "So, what do you say?" Mac's eyes pinned Cade, willing the right response from him. "I really will make it worth your while." She began to name a sum, but he seemed not to hear.

"Finding your niece will accomplish that," he informed her.

The fees were necessary for expenses, for maintaining the latest in high-tech equipment and to pay off his partners. Cade himself required very little in the way of monetary compensation. The satisfaction of being present when parents were reunited with their missing children was something priceless.

The only thing that would ever top it would be to find his own son.

Cade thought of what he'd said to Sam when Savannah King had turned to him, asking that he tell Sam that he had to take her along. He'd empathized with her, pushing Sam into agreeing. But there had been extenuating circumstances in that case. Savannah was looking for her child. The missing child they were about to search for was not McKayla Dellaventura's daughter. Mothers were one thing, aunts having rules broken for them were quite another.

Still, he supposed if he now refused this woman, it would make him a hypocrite.

He didn't like the sound of the word. Or the feel of it. Like a general in the field, he would have never asked anyone to do something he wouldn't. That included bringing along a client into the trenches.

With a sigh, he flipped his notebook to the next page and took out a tape recorder from his drawer, which he placed between them on the desk. He saw a flicker of triumph in her eyes, coupled with just the slightest touch of wariness.

At least she didn't jump to conclusions without prompting, he thought.

"I say, all right." He gestured for her to sit down again. "But I will hold you to your promise. There's to be no question as to who's in charge of the investigation." It wasn't a warning, it was a fact. The first moment she tried to take over, client or not, she would be sent away. There was good reason for him to feel that way. "I don't want you trying to get ahead of me."

Mac took her seat, appearing relaxed. "I sincerely doubt if I could."

He took it as more flattery. Flattery was window dressing meant to distract the eye and take attention away from the fact that there was nothing of substance beneath. He'd never been taken in by flattery, even when he was much younger.

"If that's supposed to lull me into a false sense of security, you needn't bother, Doctor. Of late, I have a habit of holding everything suspect."

Mac liked honesty. It was the first quality she looked for in a person and the only one she required. "Then we have something in common."

They were probably limited to that one thing, Cade thought. He sincerely doubted that there were any other traits that they shared.

"All right—" he pushed down the record button on the machine "—let's get started."

For the next hour, he fired questions at her. To her credit, Mac answered every one to the best of her knowledge, without flinching or hedging.

At first glance, if everything Mac told him was true, it seemed that they could rule out that Heather was kidnapped in order to exact revenge. And, with no ransom note in the picture, it didn't look as if whoever took her—if they took the little girl intentionally— was looking to return her.

Cade looked at his notes. What he saw, what he'd heard, was slightly baffling and rather unbelievable. It was either a daring kidnapping in broad daylight, or a strange carjacking that had gone horribly awry.

"It sounds as if your sister was deliberately run off the road."

It was the same thought Mac had been wrestling with. "But why? She doesn't have an enemy in the world. My sister volunteers at the local hospital three times a week. All the kids in the neighborhood adore her. There's no disgruntled boyfriend in the wings or offstage, no one with a grudge of any sort. Why would this happen?"

"I would say that it might have been something as simple as misplaced road rage, if your niece hadn't been taken."

Cade frowned, thinking. He'd never been an optimist by nature, but sitting in this chair, hearing the stories he'd heard, he had become acquainted with the very worst side of humanity. And it prompted him to look for the worst in a situation. Ugly possibilities were suggesting themselves to him now.

"Outside the immediate family, was anyone overly attentive to Heather?"

Mac thought before she spoke, wanting to be absolutely certain about the information she gave him. Instead of answering him, she took out her wallet and extracted Heather's photograph. It was taken at a studio less than a month ago. She placed it on the desk between them.

Cade picked it up and looked at the little girl. Dressed in a frilly pink outfit, Heather had her head thrown back, her mouth captured in a laugh that he could almost hear and felt himself tempted to share. She'd been posed with a soft, live rabbit.

Mac noted his reaction. Nothing short of what she'd expected. She'd made her point. Heather was the kind of little girl who turned people's heads. "Everyone paid attention to Heather."

"Can I keep this?"

She gestured for him to take the photograph. "Please." She noted the look on his face, and it made her uneasy. "What are you thinking?"

Cade knew she wasn't going to like it, but that wasn't the point of the investigation. She wanted the truth, and he owed it to her. "That this might have all been set up."

"Set up how?"

"Your sister might have been run off the road in order to kidnap Heather." He looked down at the photograph again. "Children like your niece are in high demand."

"Demand?" Mac didn't understand. Didn't want to understand. "By whom?"

"By couples who have no children." The reality was harsher than that. "The step before that would be the baby brokers."

"Black market babies?" She spoke incredulously.

"Maybe. Right now, this is all pure speculation." He tucked away the photograph into his pocket. "I might be completely off. The police might have already located your niece while you were telling me the details of your story.''

Though she would have loved to believe that, Mac had a sinking feeling that it was far from likely. Still, what Cade had proposed sounded too fantastic to sensibly entertain.

''But to pull that off, they'd need someone to run her off the road, ambulances, paramedics...'' She looked at him. ''It doesn't sound real.''

''There's a reason why the saying 'truth is stranger than fiction' came into being. And maybe you're right,'' he allowed. At least, they could hope. ''But for now, why don't we take it one step at a time and see if we can unravel this as we go along? Do you know the name of the ambulance company that took your niece away?''

Frustrated, Mac shook her head. She hadn't thought to ask that.

''Is your sister up to being questioned?''

That he asked rather than assumed made a good impression on Mac. ''She's up to doing anything she can to find Heather.''

''Good.''

Cade jotted down a few more notes in his pad. The crime had occurred in Newport Beach, along the Pacific Coast Highway, the PCH. He wasn't all that familiar with the department down there, but there was no time like the present to remedy that. He'd have to get in touch with the detective in charge of the investigation. Stepping on official toes was something he was very careful not to do. He'd found that professional courtesy had a fifty-fifty chance of being returned. The odds could have always been better, but a man in his profession took what he could get.

Cade raised his eyes to look at her. The stray thought that she was an exceptionally pretty woman to be the pillar for her family occurred to him. "Anything else you want to tell me?"

Several things raced through Mac's mind, but they all sounded suspiciously too close to hysteria to voice. Panic was something that she kept secretly bottled up inside her. Giving way to her own feelings of despair wouldn't do Moira or Heather any good. And probably would give Townsend the excuse he was looking for to leave her behind.

"Only that I'm willing to do anything to get my niece back as quickly as possible."

That was already understood. Cade shut off the tape recorder and then closed the notepad. He rose, tucking the notepad into his pocket. "All right, I'll see what I can find out."

Mac was back on her feet instantly, not about to give him the opportunity to leave without her. She was tall, but he was taller and had incredibly long legs.

"The agreed-upon pronoun is *we*, not *I*," she reminded him as she followed him to his door.

Cade stopped, turning to look at her. Good as her word—or threat—she appeared ready to shadow his every movement. This, he thought, could get very irritating, even for a man who had schooled himself to turn patience into almost a religion.

"Starting now?"

"Starting right now—unless you have something else to do first."

Taking a deep breath, Cade sighed. "Even a condemned man gets a last meal."

"We'll eat on the way. Part of 'expenses.' I'll pay."

No, he thought, he had a serious hunch that if there was any "paying" to be done, he would be the one doing it. In spades.

"I was talking about breathing space," he clarified. "I wasn't being literal."

Mac flushed, but recovered quickly. One of the very few women in her chosen course of study when she'd begun it, she'd had to learn how to roll with the punches and spring up quickly. It had been the only way to earn her the respect of her peers.

"My mistake," she admitted. But then her eyes pinned him. "We're going to have to get our lines of communication straight if we're going to be working together."

It was on the tip of Cade's tongue to suggest that perhaps that indicated that working together was not the best idea, but that would only embroil him in a further exchange with her. One, he had a feeling, he wasn't going to win any more than he had won the first.

Well, he decided, Dr. McKayla Dellaventura was accomplishing at least one thing. She was temporarily taking his mind off his own loss.

She was also getting under his skin, something he hadn't thought possible until just now. "C'mon," he murmured, surrendering for now.

As he walked into the outer office, Cade saw Rusty slapping Sam on the back just as Megan released him from what appeared to be a rather intense hug. From their expressions, they'd all just shared something hugely uplifting. He thought of the case Sam was working on. The natural assumption was that Sam had cracked the case.

He looked from Sam to Megan. "Something going on here I should know about?"

Whether it was the fact that she was a woman or that she went further back with Cade than the others did, Megan found that she was more in tune to Cade than either Sam or Rusty were. Though his face was impassive, she noticed the edge in his voice immediately.

Small wonder, given what today was. In a heartbeat, sympathy for Cade and what he was continuously forced to endure washed over her. Their association went back to the day she'd been called in by the Bureau to help find Darin Townsend. That the book was still opened on this abduction was something Megan never quite allowed to leave her mind.

With a bearing reminiscent of an overly large, affectionate puppy, Rusty turned to Cade to answer his question. "We're celebrating Sam's news."

Rusty, Cade knew, never took the short route when a longer one was available. "Which is?"

Sam couldn't hold it in any longer. He'd found out this morning and had gone from stunned to jubilant in record time. "We're pregnant. I mean, Savannah's pregnant, but I'm going to be a father."

"You already are a father," Megan reminded him.

"Yes, but this is different," he insisted. "This time it's from scratch."

Savannah already had a daughter. It was in reuniting the two that Sam had become such an integral part of their lives, and they of his. But this meant being there from the very beginning, an awe-inspiring prospect any way he looked at it.

"Hell, I never even had a dog before. Suddenly, I'm going to be the father of two—" Like a thunderclap sounding over his head, Sam suddenly realized what he was saying and to whom. He wouldn't have hurt Cade for the world. There weren't words enough to apologize. "Hey, I'm sorry, I didn't mean—"

But Cade shook his head. "No, that's great, really great. I'm very happy for you, Sam." And he genuinely was. He didn't want people tiptoeing around him because of the ongoing tragedy in his life. Especially not people he had gotten so close to and cared about. "I just hope the baby has the good sense to get its looks from Savannah so it doesn't stop clocks." There was affection in the grin that spread out on Cade's face. "You'll make a great father. You already know how to say yes."

Megan had ducked into her office and returned now with something she'd worked on this morning before Sam had stopped by with his announcement. Moving to his other side, she placed her hand on Cade's arm to get his attention.

"Cade, before I forget, I thought you might want this." Megan handed him a photograph fresh from her color printer.

Cade turned toward her. "What is it?" The question died in his throat as he looked at the reproduction. A bittersweet feeling twisted inside him before he blocked it.

"It's an update of what Darin would look like

now.'' Judging by the expression that came over Cade's face, Megan realized it was a needless explanation. ''I just upgraded the software.'' She caught her bottom lip between her teeth. Maybe she shouldn't have given this to him now. ''I thought it might help—''

Cade caught the hesitation in her voice. He was making her uncomfortable, he realized. Making all of them uncomfortable. ''You thought right.'' Very carefully, he folded the page and tucked it into his wallet. ''Thanks.''

''Don't mention it.'' Meagan's eyes shifted to the woman who had come in earlier. She read the body language. ''Going somewhere?'' she asked Cade.

''I'm—we're,'' he corrected himself, glancing at Mac, ''on our way out. This is Dr. McKayla Dellaventura, our newest client.'' Cade made the introductions quickly. ''Rusty Andreini, Megan Andreini. And Sam Walters, my partners.'' Without thinking, he placed his hand on the small of Mac's back, ushering her out. ''I'll be in touch,'' he promised Megan. ''Great news, Sam,'' he said again. ''Give Savannah my best.''

They all seemed to get along well, Mac thought. Desperate for assurances, she took it as a good sign. Following Cade to his car, she nodded toward the building they had just left. ''Nice people.''

''Yeah, they are.'' He unlocked the passenger door, then held it open for her. ''The best.''

She wasn't accustomed to manners that, by and large, could be termed as courtly and had fallen by the wayside in today's world. It took her a moment before she recovered and got into the car. He closed the door, then rounded the hood to his side.

There were all sorts of newly formed questions rattling around in her head. She selected one at random, since it seemed to pertain to him.

"Who's Darin?" The moment she asked, she saw Cade's jaw tighten ever so slightly. Maybe she had no business asking, but the look on his face when Megan had handed him the computer-generated photograph had instantly caught her attention.

"Darin's my son." He looked at her as he turned the key in the ignition. He wasn't sure why he was telling her this, only that in talking about his son, it somehow kept Darin alive for him. "Today is his sixth birthday. And before you ask—" he anticipated her question "—he's been missing for three years." Suddenly, Cade found himself describing that horrifying event.

He'd looked away for a minute, only a minute when that man had asked him directions. Older than Cade, the man had looked somewhat harried. There'd been a little girl, maybe four, maybe younger, tugging urgently on his arm, and Cade remembered thinking how fortunate he was with Darin. Darin who was always so well behaved.

When Cade had looked back, the kiddie train ride was over, but Darin wasn't sitting in the tiny, colorful engineer's seat. He wasn't rushing over to him, arms outstretched, bubbling over with words. Eager to share every single aspect of his new adventure.

Closing his eyes, Cade could vividly recall the sick feeling in the pit of his stomach as he began calling for Darin. Began searching.

Darin wasn't anywhere in the park.

Every last man on the security detail combed the entire park for hours after that. All they'd found was Darin's Angels cap near one of the men's rooms.

From then until now, there'd been a lot of winding roads that all led to dead ends. Thousands of "tips" called in, amounting to the same.

Cade had gone over that day, those few minutes, in his mind more than a thousand times, replaying the scenario, looking for that microscopic detail that he might have missed before. That detail that would lead him to his son.

He'd even placed an ad in the local papers, trying to find the man he'd spoken to in case the man had inadvertently seen something. But that had led him nowhere as well. There'd never been a response.

The words felt like sharp nails being driven through his heart all over again as he said them. Three years. He'd missed three years in his son's life. Three years he was never going to get back. But somehow, some way, he was going to find a way to make that up to Darin. It would begin the moment they were reunited.

The answer pulled Mac up short. She'd come to the agency because a friend of her father's had recommended it to her. Because time was so important, she hadn't stopped to familiarize herself with the background information. She twisted in her seat, straining the seat belt she'd just finished buckling. "You can't find your own son?"

Cade banked down the flash of temper he felt. "My son is why I started this agency. And to date, his is the only open case we have on our files." His foot on the brake, he held off backing out of the lot.

"Why, would you be more comfortable with another investigative agency?"

Mac's first instinct was to say yes. Her second was more analytical. The man was obviously dedicated to his work. And if their track record was as close to perfect as humanly possible, she couldn't ask for more than that.

"No. I was told that your agency is the best, and if you have only one unresolved case, then those are the best statistics I've ever heard. I'm only sorry that it has to be your own son."

"So am I," Cade replied quietly.

She looked at him. "At least you know then what my family and I are going through."

"Yes," he replied solemnly, taking his foot off the brake. "I know exactly what you're going through."

Chapter 3

"Moira, honey, it's Mac. I brought the detective with me. The one who's going to find Heather for us."

Though Cade always thought positively each time he undertook a new case, hearing the prophesy of success weighed heavily on his shoulders.

He saw what looked like a glimmer of hope flicker through the dark eyes as they shifted to focus on him. It took a moment before the resemblance actually became apparent to Cade. At first glance, the sisters looked nothing alike.

But on closer scrutiny, he saw that the pale woman who appeared to be almost swallowed up by the hospital bed she was lying in looked like a preliminary sketch of the woman standing beside him. It was as if with McKayla, all the colors had been filled in, while Moira's colors were muted, applied behind a gauzelike screen. She made him think of one of those rare flowers that wasn't expected to be able to survive outside of a controlled environment.

If the circumstances hadn't been urgent, Cade would have opted to withdraw from the private hospital room and return at some later time, when Moira looked as if she was more up to talking.

Cade smiled at Moira. "I'm Cade Townsend, Mrs. McGuire. I need to ask you some questions."

His statement was met with an annoyed huff from the man standing on the other side of Moira's bed. Gray eyes narrowed beneath tufted, grayer eyebrows. "Can't you go to the police instead?" the man demanded sharply. Concern was etched into the deep lines on his thin, angular face. "My daughter's been through a great deal, she needs her rest."

"In case you haven't guessed—" Mac turned toward Cade "—this is my father, Dr. Arthur Dellaventura. And this is my mother, Sylvia. My brother—" she indicated a younger, even taller man by the window "—Danny."

Cade nodded at each introduction in turn, but his attention was drawn to Mac's father. "I appreciate your daughter's condition, Dr. Dellaventura, but if we're to find your granddaughter, I need to get Mrs. McGuire's perspective on the incident if it's at all possible. Sometimes the smallest clue—"

"Please, Arthur," Sylvia entreated quietly, laying a hand on her husband's arm, "let him do what he has to to find Heather."

It struck Cade that Sylvia was far more like Moira than her older daughter. Almost wraithlike, both women appeared as if they needed to be looked after, cared for. McKayla hadn't given him that impression from the first word she'd uttered. Obviously, she took after her father, Cade mused.

Frowning, Arthur acquiesced to the validity of his wife's words. With a second, far more helpless, far more frustrated huff, Arthur Dellaventura waved his hand at Cade to proceed.

Cade looked at Moira. Her pupils were dilated. They'd undoubtedly pumped her full of pain medication. For her daughter's sake, he hoped she could manage to think clearly. "Can you tell me in your own words what happened?" he asked softly.

Stepping back, Mac allowed Cade better access to her sister. It killed her to see Moira this way. If she ever got her hands on the person who did this to her… One thing at a time, Mac cautioned herself silently. First they had to find Heather. She was impressed, despite the dire, urgent situation, by the way he spoke to Moira. Softly, gently, as if she were a wounded bird on the verge of dying of fright. Ever since she could remember, everyone had always treated Moira as if she were about to break. Mac was no exception. It was just the way things were.

Both Moira and her mother were cut from the same finely spun, delicate cloth. Like her brothers, Mac took after her father. She was direct and blunt, though not as blunt as Arthur could be. At times, secretly, she wished that, just for a day, she could cross the line and be like her mother and sister. See what it felt like to be taken care of, to bring out protective instincts from those around her instead of having them drawn out of herself.

But she knew that even if things could arrange

themselves so that came to pass, she'd have no patience with it after the first five minutes. She was a doer, a caregiver, not taker. She'd been that way all of her life; it was too late to change things now, and for the most part, she was satisfied with the way they were.

Confronted with Cade's question, her sister seemed to sink even further into her pillow. "Try, Moira," Mac coaxed softly. "For Heather."

Breathing heavily, Moira moistened her lips. The look on her face told Cade she was trying to piece together her scattered thoughts.

In a reed-thin voice, she began. "I was driving down PCH, the Pacific Coast Highway." She used the highway's full name, as if to make the story clearer to herself as well as to him. "We'd just left the toy store in the mall. Heather and I. Someone…someone was driving behind me. They kept coming closer, faster." Her eyes filled with tears. "I changed lanes but they kept following. And then they ran me off the road." Her voice hitched. Mac took her hand in mute support. Moira didn't seem to notice. "The car was spinning. I was screaming." Drained, she looked at Cade. He saw the fear there. "I thought we were going to die."

He didn't allow himself to be sidetracked by the emotion he was experiencing. "Did you notice the make of the car? License plate? Anything?"

Moira moved her head from side to side, frustration whispering over her pale features. "Blue. The car was blue."

So were tens of thousands of other cars on the road,

Cade thought. Not much to go on. He came to the payoff question. "Did they stop?"

"No."

But she wasn't sure, he saw it in her eyes.

"I don't think so," she amended. "It's all fuzzy." Moira struggled to remember. "There was an ambulance. Paramedics." She'd kept passing in and out, losing consciousness. "I thought Heather was there with me. They told me she was alive, but she had cuts. They were afraid that there might be internal bleeding." After that, it was all blank until she woke up in the hospital. "I'm sorry, I don't remember. I hit my head, nothing's clear."

The barest trace of color had appeared, then disappeared from her cheek when she relived the accident. The bandage across one side of her forehead looked more vivid than Moira did. Moved, Cade laid a hand over Moira's thin, translucent one.

"That's all right, ma'am. You've been very helpful." As he stepped back, Sylvia and Arthur closed ranks around their daughter's bed. Sylvia sat down, taking up her vigil again.

Mac was at Cade's side the moment he left her sister's bedside. Cade wondered if she thought he was going to ditch her somehow. The thought was tempting.

Arthur separated himself from the circle around Moira's bed for a moment. Danny took his place as Arthur approached Cade. Taking his arm, he moved with Cade to the side of the room.

The gray eyes took measure of him before the man spoke. "What do you need from us?" Though gruff, the motive behind the question was sincere.

"Nothing right now." Cade glanced at Mac. "Your other daughter has offered to provide me with all the extra help I might need." But Cade liked to keep as many options open as possible. You never knew. "If I need anything else, I'll let you know."

Arthur nodded curtly and returned to his post.

Mac waited until they were back out in the hall outside the room and past myriad relatives. She tried not to dwell on the fact that Cade had referred to her as her parents' "other" daughter. Without meaning to, he'd hit the way her parents viewed her right on the head. In comparison to Moira, she'd always been "the other one." It was something she had come to terms with, although every once in a while, like now, it managed to take her by surprise all over again.

She lengthened her stride to keep up with him. "Not much to go on, is there?"

He stopped by the elevator, pressing the down button. "I've worked with less."

Mac turned toward him, lowering her voice though there was no one around other than Cade to hear her. "You don't have to sugarcoat things, Mr. Townsend, I'm the strong one. I prefer the truth."

The strong one. Was she comparing herself to her sister, or to everyone in her family? Cade had a hunch it might very well be the latter.

"The truth is that I have worked with less," he repeated.

"Successfully?" she challenged, unwilling to be patronized. If she was going to grasp onto hope, she wanted at least a nylon thread of provocation.

The elevator arrived. He let her enter first. "Yes." Cade pressed for the lobby.

Mac stared at the steel-gray doors as they closed. "All right, what's our next move?" But before he could answer, she said, "Because I thought that we might talk to the ambulance drivers who brought her here—"

"That's our next move."

Their eyes held for a second. Long enough for Mac to feel something like confidence seeping into her. She smiled. "Told you I wouldn't get in the way."

Yeah, right. Her very presence was beginning to get in the way. In subtle ways Cade hadn't been prepared for. He blocked out things he couldn't waste time with exploring at the moment.

The doors parted and they got off, making their way through a crowd of people, all determined to use the same car to reach their destination.

"Did your sister mention that anyone suspicious was hanging around her?" Seeing the puzzled look in her eyes, he elaborated. "Calling her on the phone at odd hours, maybe 'bumping' into her more times than might be thought of as coincidental?"

"You mean like stalking her?" When he nodded, Mac stifled a shiver at the thought of someone slinking after her sister like that, lying in wait, shadowing Moira's moves. "No."

"Are you sure?" Cade stopped to read the signs at the corner, pointing in various directions. Administration was to the right.

Mac found herself hurrying to keep up. "Yes, I'm sure. Moira would have mentioned it if there were. She tells me everything. Moira tends to be a little on the timid side."

She was given to understatement as well as being

a steamroller. A smile played on Cade's lips for a moment, softening the sun-bronzed, angular features that had come to him via his grandmother's Cherokee bloodlines. "Doesn't take up sword and shield, the way you do, eh?"

Mac didn't know if he was laughing at her or not. She dismissed the question, by saying, "I'm older."

Cade seriously doubted that age had anything to do with it. It was temperament and outlook that dictated the differences, not age, but that wasn't his concern. Only finding Heather was.

The redheaded clerk in the administration office was more than eager to help in any way she could. She gave them the name of the ambulance company, all the while assuring them that nothing like this had *ever* happened before in Harris Memorial's seventy-three-year history.

Sensing what motivated her agitation, Mac assured the woman that her family wasn't looking to bring any legal action against the hospital. The administration supervisor appeared visibly relieved.

"It's a dog-eat-dog world," Mac said in response to Cade's raised brow as they left the office. "People are too eager to sue everyone for everything these days."

"Are you speaking for yourself, or your family right now?" Cade asked. Had the family practice been sued? Was there perhaps a disgruntled former patient seeking twisted revenge behind the kidnapping?

"Both." It wasn't the hospital's fault what had happened to Moira, any more than it was Moira's fault for driving off the road to begin with, Mac thought. A look at his face told Mac what he was thinking. "And no, we've never been sued. Not even close."

She was good. Damn good, Cade thought with admiration as he drove to the ambulance company that had brought Moira McGuire to Harris Memorial. Mercy Ambulance's office was just off the Pacific Coast Highway.

On the way, Mac pointed out the site of Moira's accident. Cade took his foot off the accelerator and steered his car toward the same side of the road.

"Think there might be something here?"

He doubted it, but there was always a chance. "Maybe." Cade opened the car door. The road, so crowded at times that traffic would come to a complete standstill, was fairly empty now. Just as it had been, he surmised from what McKayla had told him, at the time of Moira's accident. "You can stay in the car. This shouldn't take long."

But as he got out, Mac followed suit on her side. He had a feeling she would.

Cade sighed quietly as he reached into the back seat for his camera. It looked as if McKayla Dellaventura meant to live up to her word. For all intents and purposes, he had himself a shadow for the duration of the investigation.

Or until it got dangerous, he thought, walking up to the skid marks on the road. The first sign of real trouble and he was sending her on her way, no matter what kind of argument she tendered.

Squatting, Cade studied the ground. The tires' skid tracks were still fresh where Moira's sedan had gone careering up the side of the road. He was working on a hunch. Maybe the other driver had meant only to frighten her, not to cause a serious accident.

Standing over him, Mac looked at the ground. The tire tracks stood out against the sun and traffic-faded asphalt. She didn't see anything of particular significance. Maybe if she got closer.

She crouched down beside him, but still saw nothing to capture his attention. But then, he was the professional. "What are you looking for?"

"Just pieces of the puzzle." Rising, he aimed his instant camera at the ground and snapped twice. He put his hand out and waited for the camera to spit out the photographs.

No debris, he noted. No extraneous parts lying in the road. Glancing at the photographs before he pocketed them, he looked at Mac. "How badly was the car damaged?"

Mac shrugged. "I don't know." Cade had turned on his heel and was walking back to the car. She hurried to catch up. "I didn't see it. The police had a tow truck take it away. Danny tracked it down and had it towed over to our mechanic's shop." Obviously, this was important. "Want his number?"

Cade tossed the camera on the back seat before getting behind the wheel. "Yes."

Getting in, Mac took a card out of one of the zippered compartments in her purse. Cade started the car again. Once they were on the road again, he took the card from her.

"Thanks." The woman was incredibly organized, he thought, slipping the card into his pocket next to the photographs. Most women of his acquaintance, outside of Megan, weren't. Organized and sexy. Not a bad combination.

"What does it matter what condition the car's in?"

"Maybe nothing," he conceded. Pressing down on the accelerator, Cade picked up speed. They just made it through a yellow light. "On the other hand, it might confirm whether or not the other driver was intentionally following your sister and just wanted to run her off the road so that he or she could kidnap Heather."

"Well, Moira did drive off the road. If that was their intention, why didn't they just grab the baby then? Why wait? And how does the other ambulance figure into all this?"

He wasn't accustomed to talking out his ideas, or having to field a volley of questions coming straight at him. Usually, he let his hunches simmer in his mind until a few more pieces came into play.

Cade spared her a glance. "I don't know—yet."

Despite his mild tone, Mac detected an edge to his words. "Don't get annoyed, I'm only trying to get ideas moving back and forth here."

Cade was very aware of what she was trying to do. And of the by-product she was creating. Even Elaine had complained about how closed-mouth he often was. If he wasn't accustomed to sharing his thoughts, he was even less accustomed to experiencing a flicker of annoyance.

So he tempered his response, turning toward amusement as he turned down the next block. "I thought I was in charge."

"You are, but I'm not a mute." Silence was not a medium she could deal with.

Cade laughed softly to himself. Among other attributes, the woman truly did have a gift for understatement. "No, that you are not."

They had their answer to Mac's question when they finally got the opportunity to question the paramedics who had taken Moira to the hospital.

On a break, the two men were found in a claustrophobic room at the back of the Mercy Ambulance's office building. The room served as a combination kitchen, dining and recreational area. The men were sitting at a table that had seen better decades, playing cards.

After introducing himself and Mac, and explaining why they were there, Cade asked, "Who called you to the scene of the accident?"

The men exchanged looks. The taller of the two stopped rocking on the rear legs of the chair and leaned forward. The front legs made contact with the floor with a jarring noise.

"Nobody."

That didn't make any sense. "Then what were you doing there?" Mac beat Cade to the question.

His curiosity about the answer was greater than his need to remind Mac about their agreement, so Cade held his tongue.

"We were driving back from making another run," the taller man said. "Saw the whole thing. This blue Camry—"

"Maxima," his partner corrected him in an irritating, high-pitched voice.

The first paramedic, Jake, according to the name stitched over his pocket, looked across the table, clearly annoyed. "It was a Camry," he insisted. "My brother works in a garage, I ought to know my cars—"

His partner, Andy, made a disparaging sound. "Just because your brother—"

Cade held up a hand, stopping the men before the questioning could degenerate into a heated argument. "This blue car, what about it?"

Jake took up his narrative. "It ran into the Camaro, ramming it. Not hard, mind you. It shouldn't have spun out of control the way it did, but I think the woman probably panicked—"

Cade noticed that Mac was struggling to keep from interrupting. He wondered how long she could refrain. "Did the driver of the other car attempt to stop?"

"Yeah, he did," Andy remembered, obviously eager to put in his two cents' worth. And then he shrugged his broad shoulders. "At least, his car slowed down. But it picked up speed again when he heard the siren."

"Siren?" Cade asked. Had the police arrived on the scene that quickly? There was a solitary house overlooking that section of the road. Had someone been watching from the window and called the police?

A superior expression creased Jake's face as he nodded toward his partner. "Andy likes to turn on the siren every chance he gets. Doesn't seem to care that he's destroying my ears."

"So the other driver just kept going?" Cade prodded, directing their attention back to the accident.

Andy nodded vigorously. He stubbed out his cigarette. "Like a bullet."

Waving away the smoke from the cigarette, Jake hissed through his teeth. "Bullets don't drive—"

Mac felt as if she were back refereeing her brothers when they were all little. She raised her voice. "Then what happened?"

"We got the woman and the baby out of the car. Andy brought the stretcher over and went to get another one for the baby, but I thought maybe the baby should go to Mission. They've got that special trauma unit, so I called them."

"No, you didn't," Andy corrected him. "I did."

Caught, Jake frowned. "Right, he did."

"How badly injured was the baby?" Cade asked. "Bump on the head and a bruise just underneath," Andy told him. "But you don't want to take chances when they're that young."

"Happen to know what ambulance company answered the call?" Cade asked, hoping to get a reply without having to listen to any more bickering between the two men.

"Yeah." Jake grabbed the pack of cigarettes off the table before his partner could reach for another one. "Dominion. They got there in less than fifteen minutes, then we took off. The cops cleaned up the rest."

"When did the police get there?" Mac asked, surprising Cade.

Andy thought. "Five, ten minutes before we left."

Cade finished jotting notes down and flipped his pad closed. "Where's Dominion located?"

"Laguna somewhere." Jake exchanged looks with

Andy, but the latter had nothing to volunteer. "Joan has the address up front." He jerked a thumb toward the front of the building.

Thanking them for their time, Cade and Mac went to get Dominion's address. In the background, they heard Jake and Andy beginning to argue again, this time over whose turn it was to deal the cards.

"It's a wonder they reached the hospital with my sister at all," Mac murmured.

Cade only laughed.

Less than five minutes later, they were back out in the small parking lot, getting into Cade's car. Mac figured she'd held on to her tongue long enough. This man was definitely not forthcoming. "So?"

Cade knew she was asking for his conclusions. He hadn't any. What he had were just deeper suspicions. "So it's beginning to look more and more as if the driver of that blue car meant to run your sister off the road to steal the baby."

Mac wasn't a Pollyanna. Mac knew what the world was like. But it was still difficult for Mac to believe that things like this were actually planned. "But they drove off—"

"When the ambulance arrived to interfere with their plans," he pointed out. "And the other ambulance is still missing."

She started to ask what he thought that meant and then stopped. He probably would only give her a nebulous answer. It was obvious that Cade Townsend didn't like being pinned down. Mac reminded herself that she was paying him for his expertise and not his company.

With a sigh, she sank back in her seat, trying not to fidget inwardly.

"I'll tell you what I already told the police. Henry and Smithy are two of our best drivers." The bald-headed man behind the counter frowned at Cade. The telephone rang, interrupting him. "Get that, will you, Billy?" he called over his shoulder to someone behind the drawn curtain that separated the medical supply showroom from its stockroom. The man turned to look at Cade and Mac again. "Henry's been with the company since it started. Smithy came on board three years ago, just before I did. If either of them are mixed up in anything underhanded here, then I'm Elvis Presley."

Another line on the telephone rang. Not bothering to hide his annoyance, the man jerked up the receiver without excusing himself.

"Dominion." A moment later, his eyes widened sufficiently enough to catch Cade's attention. "Are they all right? And the ambulance?" He breathed a loud sigh of relief as Cade and Mac exchanged looks. "Thank God. Sure, thanks, and thanks for calling, Officer."

The man hung up, his face a mask of triumph. "That was the police department. They just found Henry and Smithy," he announced. "And the missing ambulance."

It was a lucky break. "Where are they?" Cade asked.

"Hey, Billy," he called out behind him before answering Cade. "Henry and Smithy are okay." Only then did he address the question. "The police just took them to Harris Memorial."

"Get the feeling we're going around in circles?" Mac muttered under her breath as they hurried out the door again.

"At least we're moving," Cade pointed out.

He was right. This certainly beat sitting in Moira's hospital room, holding her sister's hand and wondering if the police had found Heather.

"Hey, I'm not complaining." Mac got into the car.

Cade nodded as if taking the information in. "Just so it's clear."

One step closer, Mac told herself as Cade started the car. *One step closer to Heather.*

Chapter 4

"But I already told all this to the police."

Buttoning his shirt, John Smith, Smithy to the immediate world, seemed in a hurry to get out of the hospital emergency room.

Glancing over toward Henry, who appeared in better shape than he was, Smithy was ready to go. "Look, I want to get home to my wife. Can't you just talk to the police and get whatever information you need?"

Cade had worked his way past a witness's reluctance to talk more often than he could remember, but before he could say anything, Mac was cornering the paramedic.

"You know as well as anybody that the police are very closemouthed when it comes to their investigations. They don't exactly believe in the buddy system. That little girl you were bringing to Mission Hospital was—is—" she corrected herself tersely, damning herself for her slip "—my niece Heather. We haven't heard a single word about her since she was taken. My sister—her mother—is in this hospital right now—in the intensive care unit." She paused deliberately, her eyes pinning the man, searching for compassion. "She needs something to hang on to." Mac placed her hand lightly on the man's forearm, her eyes still on his. "Help me give it to her."

Watching her, Cade couldn't help but wonder just how much of what she'd said to him earlier had been true and how much had been fabrication. There was no denying that she could turn in a performance on demand.

Smithy ran his hand through his thinning dark hair and sighed. "Okay, I guess I can spare another five minutes." He looked at his partner again. "How about you, Henry?"

A wiry man, somewhat taller and younger than Smithy, Henry crossed to the bed his partner was still sitting on. "Okay by me."

Triumphant, Mac forged on, completely forgetting about the man at her side. "What did he look like—the person driving the Camry?"

Smithy looked at her in confusion for a minute. "It wasn't a he, it was a she."

"A woman?" Cade raised an eyebrow in surprise, glancing toward Mac. They had both assumed, just the way the other set of ambulance drivers had, that Heather's abductor was a man.

Smithy, the more vocal of the two, elaborated. "Yeah, a really well-dressed one, too. She got into the ambulance with us. With me," he clarified, since

Henry was in the front, driving. "She said she was the baby's aunt. That she'd been in the car when the accident happened. Said her sister wanted her to go with the baby." He looked from Mac to Cade. "In all the excitement, I didn't think anything of it. I figured, why not?"

Henry said something unintelligible under his breath, then cleared his throat, looking at Smithy. "I guess we won't be taking extra passengers along any time soon after this."

The chagrined look on Smithy's face indicated he was in agreement with the driver.

"What happened?" Cade prodded.

"As soon as we drove away from the scene of the accident, the woman took out a gun, pointed the damn thing at me and yelled to Henry to drive to an out-of-the-way place along the western stretch of PCH."

"Huntington Beach," Henry interjected.

A nurse came and politely asked them to adjourn the discussion to the another section of the room. The bed was needed for another patient.

Reining in her impatience, Mac waited until they reached the first available empty space. "And then what?"

"She made Henry stop, then had him tie me up," Smithy resumed. "I asked her what she wanted, but this woman, she didn't talk just to talk, she just gave orders, nothing more. After knocking me unconscious, she apparently tied Henry up and got out with the baby."

"She wouldn't just walk off," Mac said, thinking out loud. "She had to have a car waiting nearby."

The kidnapping was beginning to take on elaborate

proportions, going in directions that made her blood run cold. How long had these people been watching Moira, waiting for their chance? And how often did this kind of thing go on?

"She did," Smithy confirmed. "She called some cab company on her cell phone after she was finished with us, told them to come and pick her up. One cool woman." Despite the situation, there was a note of admiration in the man's voice.

"Did either of you happen to see the cab?" Mac pressed. She knew it was an extreme long shot.

"I did." Smithy smiled, exposing one gleaming gold tooth. "I got up on my knees and looked out the back window just as she was going in."

"What kind of a cab?" Cade asked.

But this time, the man shook his head. "Couldn't make out the name. But it was yellow. Had a big sign on the top advertising that new play. The one at the Center." Unable to recall the name, he looked from Mac to Cade, frustrated. "My wife wants to go see it." His mind was a blank. "You know, the one with the guy in the mask. Ghost something."

"Phantom of the Opera?" Mac guessed, unable to think of anything else.

Smithy slapped his hands together, then pointed two fingers triumphantly at Mac. "That's the one."

"Anything else?" Cade asked.

Smithy shook his head. "That's all. Does it help?"

"It helps," Cade assured him. Everything helped. It would take some doing, tracking down the cab, but at least they had something to work with. He pushed his luck, trying to get a little more. "Where did the police finally find you?"

This time, Smithy looked to Henry for an answer.

"Can't say, exactly. She had me driving for a while, turning down long stretches of isolated road. Just know it was by the ocean somewhere in Huntington Beach."

They'd been missing for more than a day. "Couldn't you yell for help?"

Henry shook his head. "She used bandages and tape to gag us. And she knew her knots. Checked us both out before she left. Had us tied up better than Thanksgiving turkeys."

"What did she look like?" Cade asked.

"That's the funny thing," Smithy told them. "The woman looked like a class act. Seeing her on the street, you'd have never thought she'd be mixed up in something like this."

More and more, Cade was beginning to think that they were up against an organization. This sounded far too professional for a random snatch, and it certainly wasn't something that had been undertaken on impulse. He wondered just how many people were involved and how intricate the network actually was.

He looked at Smithy. "Do you think you could go into a little more detail about the woman?"

"She was tall—taller than you," he added, looking at Mac. "Blond, maybe around forty or so, but really well taken care of. Great figure. Had on one of those outfits—you know the kind." He searched his mind for the right word. "My wife calls 'em powder suits, something like that."

"Power suits?" Mac suggested.

"Yeah, that's the word." He grinned again, as if

he'd hit a bull's-eye. "She had a real pretty face. Like a Valentine."

"Heart-shaped?" Mac suggested.

Out of the corner of her eye, she saw Cade writing more things down in his notepad. She felt impatience scurrying, going nowhere, like tiny hamster paws leaving tracks on a vinyl floor.

Smithy's shoulders rose and fell spasmodically. He bit off a groan, massaging one. Being tied up for more than a day had left its mark.

"Damn, that hurts." He looked at Cade. "I don't know what it's called."

An idea suddenly occurred to Mac. "Do you think you could describe her to a sketch artist?" she asked the paramedic eagerly.

A dour expression nudged his smile aside. Smithy had already given them more time than he'd intended. "How long is *that* going to take?"

Cade countered the man's question with another. "How long will it take your conscience to stop making you feel guilty if this little girl is never returned to her mother?" he asked quietly.

When Cade put it that way, Smithy felt he and Henry had no choice. He answered for both of them. "We'll talk to the sketch artist."

Since she suggested it, Cade figured Mac could follow through. "Have anyone in mind?"

Even as he asked, Mac was already taking out her cell phone. She hit a single number, then pressed the send button. "My brother Randy was born with a brush in his hand."

"My sympathies to your mother," Cade murmured.

She flashed him a smile that Cade found more than mildly distracting. Just like the woman herself.

"Is this what you mean?"

Randy Dellaventura held up his sketch pad for the two men to view. He had started from scratch three times in the last twenty-five minutes, going back to the beginning to try to capture the elusive woman who seemed to have left very different impressions on the paramedics.

It took a while, with a maximum of erasures and compromises, before the two men could finally come to some sort of agreement.

"Yeah, that's her all right." Satisfied, Smithy looked up at Cade. "Told you she was a class act."

With a weary, pleased sigh, Randy tore off the sketch and surrendered it to the man his family had hired to find his niece.

Cade studied it for a moment. The woman didn't look like anyone he had come across in his line of work. But the octopus that was the black-market baby ring was always growing new tentacles.

He turned the sketch toward Mac. There was still a chance that the kidnapper might be someone familiar to her family. "Look like anyone you might know?"

She'd watched every stroke that Randy had made, hoping. But now she shook her head. It wasn't going to be that easy, Mac thought.

Cade glanced toward Randy. He caught himself wondering how many more there were in the family. He'd grown up an only child in a quiet, proper home. He had a feeling that the Dellaventura homestead was anything but quiet during those same years. Not if Mac had been a part of it.

"Nice work." The first chance he got, Cade meant to feed the sketch into a scanner. There was a database set up on the Web for this kind of information. Besides that, he was going to need copies to pass around.

But first things first.

"We need to have your sister take a look at this," he told Mac and Randy.

"No." Moira shook her head, handing the sketch back to Cade. "I never saw this woman before. Is she the one who took Heather?"

"We think so," Cade told her gently.

"But why? Why would someone do something so terrible? Why would they take my little girl?" Moira's eyes filled up with tears again. She wiped away the ones that spilled out. "I thought I'd already cried all the tears out."

"We'll make her pay for this, Moira," Mac said fiercely. "I promise you that. Now pull yourself together and get well. You can't take care of Heather from a hospital bed." She squeezed Moira's hand. "I'll see you later." Turning toward Cade, she nodded toward the door. "Okay, let's go."

She was giving him orders again, Cade thought. Apparently the woman didn't know how to take a back seat. He followed her out, but once they were in the hall, he stopped dead. When she looked at him impatiently, he asked, "Go where?"

For a second, Mac wasn't sure what he was saying,

or why he was asking her. She waved a hand vaguely in the air. "To the next place."

Cade crossed his arms before his chest, waiting. It'd be interesting to see what she came up with. "Which is?"

What was he doing? "I don't know, you're the detective."

"Exactly. Try to remember that for more than three seconds at a time." His point made, he headed toward the elevator bank.

"Sorry." Mac struggled to hold on to her temper, goaded by impatience, as she hurried after him. "I had no idea you were that sensitive."

"I'm not. Generally." He pushed the down button, then looked at her. "How're your telephone skills?"

"Excuse me?"

He just grinned as the elevator arrived and they got in.

Mac didn't have long to wait for her explanation.

They returned to his office. A temp named Audra who Megan had brought in was manning the phones, taking messages. The others were out, Audra informed him when Cade asked after their whereabouts, working on their separate cases.

"You like being on top of the situation as much as I do," Mac commented to his back.

"It's not quite the same thing." Finding what he was looking for, Cade turned around, a thick telephone directory in his hands. "I run the agency. It's my job to know where everyone is. C'mon." He led the way to his office. "You can use the phone in here. I'll be across the hall in Megan's office."

A slight sting pricked at her before she asked, ''I annoy you that much?''

She'd lost him. ''What?''

''Why the separate offices?''

''Because we need two phones. You can take line one, I'll take line two.'' He passed a directory to her. ''First order of business is to call the local hospitals to see if anyone brought a little girl fitting Heather's description into the emergency room yesterday. There're five in the area.''

''I'll call them.''

''After that, call the cab companies listed on the first page. I'll take page two.'' He knew Megan kept her own copy of the yellow pages in her office. ''Ask—''

''If they picked up a fare with a little girl in the Huntington Beach vicinity yesterday morning,'' she supplied.

He had to admit, albeit a bit grudgingly, that he did like the way her mind worked. ''Ahead of me as usual,'' he quipped.

She wasn't about to apologize for having a quick mind. Mac thought of it as her only asset. ''That does annoy you, doesn't it?''

''Not particularly.'' He had to be honest. ''Having you finish my sentences, however, does.'' Lingering even though he knew he shouldn't, he smiled at her. The woman had very expressive eyes. If he watched them, he could almost see what she was thinking. The key word here, he thought, was *almost*. ''I admire a quick mind.''

''Just not on a woman.''

He paused. He wondered if being defensive came

naturally to her, or if something had made her that way. "You're not as good at reading people as you think, Dr. Dellaventura. Megan Andreini is one of my closest friends. Last time I checked, she was both a female and a damn sharp human being. I wouldn't have taken her on as a partner if she wasn't."

"Then it's just me," Mac concluded. Without realizing it, she hugged the directory to her chest. "I have a habit of rubbing people the wrong way."

She *was* being defensive, Cade thought. And maybe just a bit vulnerable. "You don't rub me the wrong way, Mac," he said quietly. "I'm just not accustomed to working with a partner."

"But you just said—"

He hadn't been clear, he realized. "Megan's my partner in the agency. But we don't live in each other's pockets. She works her cases. I work mine. Sometimes we pick each other's brains. But we don't make field trips together. This is an entirely new experience for me. You'll have to cut me a little slack." He nodded at the directory she held against her. "Yell if you come up with something."

She looked down at the telephone book. More time was going to go by. Time they didn't have. "Wouldn't the police already have this information?"

"Maybe, maybe not. They might be doing exactly what we are at this stage of the investigation. And even if they were ahead, I don't know the detective working this." He'd gotten a name, but he had no association, no history and no one who knew someone who knew someone who knew the detective. In this case, there were no degrees of separation to fall back on. "In order to pick a brain, you have to be familiar with that brain.'' He tapped the phone book. ''Start calling.''

Resigned, Mac walked over to the desk and sat down, then flipped the directory open to the *C*s.

Mac drew a line through another name on the page. That made fifteen calls. Fifteen strikeouts. Nothing but dead ends.

Tired, she rotated her neck, then lifted her hair off it and massaged the tense cramps that were forming. She struggled to hold a feeling of growing despair at bay. She needed to refuel.

There'd been a pot of coffee in the waiting area when they'd walked into the office. Maybe that would help recharge her.

Getting up, she walked across the hall to the office Cade was in. Megan's office. Mac noticed the slight feminine touches here and there, but mostly, the office was utilitarian. Like Cade's. She wondered if the word *partner* had a deeper meaning for the two.

Cade looked up just as she popped her head in, a silent question in his eyes. Moving her head from side to side, Mac jerked her thumb toward the hall. ''Is that coffee for anyone?''

On hold, Cade was waiting while the person on the other end of the line checked the various driver logs for the previous day. He tucked the receiver against his neck and shoulder. ''Help yourself.''

''Thanks.'' She took a step out, then stopped. ''You want any?''

''Sounds good.'' He thrived on coffee. The stronger the better. ''Black, no sugar.''

Just the thought of that made her shiver. "Sounds more like penance than coffee."

She took plenty of cream and sugar in hers. It was the caffeine she required, but it had to go down smooth. Since Heather had been kidnapped, it felt to Mac as if she'd been going strictly on coffee. Exhaustion would come, then go, chased away by a wave of fresh coffee. So far, it was Mac two, exhaustion nothing. She hadn't slept more than a few minutes in two days, but eventually, Mac knew she was going to crash.

Returning with two mugs, she placed Cade's in front of him on the desk. "One cup of mud," she announced.

Raising his eyes to hers, Cade nodded his thanks. His attention was focused on the voice on the other end of the line.

"Is he there now? Any chance we can talk to him? We can be there in—" he paused, looking at the address he'd circled in the book "—twenty minutes. Right. No problem."

Eager, Mac wanted to tug on his arm, but she waited until Cade hung up. The instant he did, she fairly pounced on him. "Did you find him?"

Cade jotted the number down on a separate piece of paper. "Looks that way."

She was at his elbow as he headed for the door. "What's 'no problem'?"

Cade tucked the address into his back pocket. "The dispatcher said we couldn't keep the driver tied up too long."

Excitement began building up inside her. She'd

been right to hire him. "Just long enough for him to tell us where he dropped that woman off."

David Hutton scratched a day-old beard and stared at the sketch for less than a second. He'd already told them that he had picked her up on the side of the road and had appeared surprised when they'd mentioned an ambulance. He hadn't taken note of any in the area.

"Yeah, that's her. I never forget a face." He handed the sketch back to Cade. "But she was smiling. And talking to the baby."

When they found her, Mac promised herself, she was going to pull every hair out of the woman's head. Heather had been in the accident along with Moira. Was injured enough for the first set of paramedics to call in another ambulance. There was no telling how bad Heather's condition actually was.

"How was the baby?" Mac asked him.

The cab driver shrugged. He hadn't noticed anything out of the ordinary, although his attention had been centered on the woman. "I don't know, like a baby, I guess. I don't know all that much about babies. This one was real quiet."

"Quiet?" Mac didn't like the sound of that. Heather was a lively, active baby.

"Yeah, like she was sleeping. The woman said she was a very good baby." He folded the fifty-dollar bill Cade had just given him, growing uncomfortable. "What's this all about, anyway?"

"The baby was kidnapped," Cade told him.

The driver's leathery face was a mask of surprise. "From that woman?"

"*By* that woman," Mac corrected him tersely.

A low whistle came between teeth that badly needed straightening. "No kidding."

Cade took out a second fifty, holding it aloft when the driver reached for it. "No kidding. Where did you take her?"

"The Bedford Chandler." He smiled as Cade placed the fifty in his palm and his fingers closed around the bill quickly as if he were afraid that Cade would decide his answers weren't worth the money.

Cade knew Mac was concerned about Heather's condition. For the kidnapper to go to a doctor, though, would be difficult, arousing suspicions not easily fielded. There would be questions to answer and forms to fill out.

"Are you thinking what I'm thinking?" Mac asked.

He nodded. "The hotel is near the airport."

"You're thinking what I'm thinking." Turning on her heels, Mac was already out the door when Cade caught up to her.

He saw the expression on her face. She obviously thought they were close to recovering Heather. It was rare, in his experience, that cases were resolved so quickly. There were usually a great many red herrings to weed out first.

He wondered if she could stand the disappointment if this lead petered out.

"You know," Cade pointed out, "she might not still be there. Or she might have used the address to throw people off in case they tracked her this far."

He was the professional, Mac thought. There was more than a chance that he was right, but she didn't want to think about it. She had to believe that she was close to getting Heather back. She couldn't face Moira again, not until she could bring Heather to her.

"Or maybe she got overconfident."

"Maybe."

He hurried to keep up with her, knowing that she was capable of running headlong into the situation. Being McKayla Dellaventura's guardian angel had just been added to Cade's list of responsibilities.

Chapter 5

"I'm sorry, we do not give out the room numbers or the names of our guests." The clerk behind the front desk of the Bedford Chandler gave them a disapproving look as he waved away the sketch Cade had taken out.

"This guest stole a baby," Mac informed him, barely curtailing her anger.

The man looked surprised. "That child wasn't hers?"

Mac pounced on his words like a prize-winning mouser on a cornered rodent. "Then she *is* here."

"Not is, was," the clerk corrected her, still a little uncertain about how on-the-level this story was. "She checked out late last night. Seemed in a hurry to go. Said she missed her husband."

"Did she happen to tell you where this husband was?" Cade pressed.

The clerk shook his head. "No."

"What about telephone calls?" Cade asked. "Did she make any from her room?"

The clerk shrugged, still unwilling to pull up the data. "I wouldn't know, although most people do."

Mac reached across the desk, laying her hand on his arm. "Can we get a look at the telephone records?"

The dour expression was back in place on the clerk's face. "That is highly irregular—"

"So's kidnapping," Mac pointed out. She took out her checkbook. "What will it take to see them?"

Glancing around to see if anyone was nearby, he leaned slightly in Mac's direction. "The baby was really kidnapped?"

They were getting somewhere, Mac thought in relief. "She's my niece. That woman who stayed here ran my sister's car off the road. She stole my sister's baby while my sister lay bleeding. She's in intensive care right now, clinging to life by a thread. Won't you please help me bring her baby back to her?"

Clearly moved, the clerk typed something into the computer. "Give me a minute," he told her with compassion as he began to scroll down the page.

Finding what he wanted, he hit the print button. The printer on the counter behind him came to life, humming softly until it spit out the completed page.

It was done in less than half a minute. The clerk placed the list in front of Mac with a flourish.

"On the house."

Standing behind her, Cade looked over Mac's shoulder at the list of telephone numbers. Her hair brushed against his cheek and he tried not to take note

of the slight tingle of electricity that snaked through
his body. Moving his head away, he focused on the
paper.

According to the sharp letters on top, the woman
who had occupied room number 824 had been named
Susan Wiley, from Seattle, Washington. Cade had his
doubts that either the name or the address she'd given
the hotel were genuine.

There were four phone calls on the printout. The
last number was a local one, the other three were
long-distance calls to the same number.

"Area code look familiar to you?" she asked, looking over her shoulder at Cade.

"No." But the moment he denied it, something in
his head nudged at a distant recollection. "Wait a
minute." Picking up the sheet, Cade studied the first
three digits, trying to crystallize the memory. "This
is Phoenix, I think."

Raising his eyes to the desk clerk, Cade saw no
confirmation or denial.

The clerk had already turned down Mac's initial
bribe, but he was about to ask for something larger
in magnitude than a room number or a telephone
printout. Cade took measure of the clerk and decided
that the man could be flexible if the inspiration were
right. Gently, he elbowed Mac aside, taking over the
counter.

"How much would it take for you to give me her
charge card number?"

"I'm afraid you're out of luck," he said, shaking
his head. And by his expression, it was apparent that
the clerk felt he was, too. His eyes widened as he saw
a fifty dollar bill being taken out. And then he sighed

at the lost opportunity. "She paid for everything with cash."

Tucking away the fifty, Cade exchanged it for a twenty and placed it on the counter as payment. The man had been as helpful as he could be—and he hadn't tried to string it out. That was worth something.

"And that didn't strike you as a little odd?" Cade asked him.

The man quickly concealed the twenty beneath his short, stubby fingers like a spider obliterating its prey. "Hey, we get odd people at the Chandler all the time, same as the other hotels." He tucked the bill into his trouser pocket. "Besides, she looked very respectable."

"So we've been told. Best kind of cover," Cade murmured. He glanced at Mac. She seemed to be holding up well. Better than he would have guessed someone in her position would have. "Where's the nearest public telephone?"

The clerk pointed to an alcove just off the main lobby.

"Thanks." With a nod in his direction, Cade crossed to the phones, found one that wasn't being used and called the one local number on their list.

Three rings later a personable voice said, "U.S. Airlines. If you'd like to make a reservation, please press—"

Just as he thought. Now at least he had the airline's name. Hanging up, Cade cut off the recording.

"Well?" Mac demanded the moment he'd hung up the receiver.

"She flew out on U.S. Airlines."

It gave them an airline, now he needed to verify the destination. The calls to Phoenix would suggest she'd gone there, but he was taking nothing for granted. Cade glanced at his watch. No wonder he was beginning to feel tired. It was getting late. He'd put in more than a full day on this. Outside, the world had long since slipped into its black, velvety case. There were still things he wanted to do, but Mac didn't figure into them.

"Maybe we should call it a night and start fresh in the morning."

He wanted to quit? Now? Struggling, Mac curbed the agitation that threatened to burst out. Instead, she marshaled her self-control and nodded.

"Fine, I'll fill you in then." Turning away from the small cluster of telephones, she headed for the revolving door in the front of the building.

Stunned, Cade hesitated half a second before he realized that she was walking away from him. Taking long strides, he caught up to her before she managed to leave the hotel. His hand on her shoulder, he turned her around. "What do you mean, fill me in?"

With a slight lift of her shoulders, she shrugged off his hand and went through the revolving door. "On what I find out," she called out.

He joined her at the curb, but she was no longer paying attention to Cade. Her destination was uppermost in her mind.

Seeing the valet, Mac waved at him, pointing the five-dollar bill tucked between her second and third fingers straight up. The pubescent man dressed in dark green livery hurried over to her. She handed him the money. "I need a cab, please."

Exasperation, quickly losing its foreign status within Cade's range of experience, pushed its way forward again. "No, she doesn't." Matching the five she'd handed out, Cade waved the man away.

Befuddled, but very obviously pleased, the valet smiled at the unexpected windfall. Pocketing the two bills, he looked hopefully from the animated woman to the tall man beside her.

"Anything else I can't get for you?" The look Cade gave him had the valet quitting while he was ahead and retreating.

"What did you do that for?" Mac demanded hotly. If she was still trying to curb her impatience, she was having no luck at it.

"Because you don't need a cab."

She frowned, her annoyance clearly showing in her eyes. "I'm not too sure what part of the country you come from, but for me, it's too far to walk."

"You're going to the airport, aren't you?"

The smile on her lips had no emotional backup. "I guess that's why you're so good at your job."

The woman was a severe test to his patience and good manners, Cade thought. Right now, he was just barely passing. With a sigh, he took her arm. "C'mon, I'll take you over."

"I'm not twelve years old," she pointed out, trying to shrug off the hold he had on her. This time, she failed. "I don't have to be dragged."

"Being twelve has nothing to do with it," he assured her.

He maintained his hold on her arm until they reached his car. The last thing he wanted was to have her run off on his watch. The case was his, and as long as it was, he wanted to keep casualties to a minimum. Cade had a feeling that the woman who took Heather wasn't operating alone and that the participants in this little drama were a great deal more sophisticated than they'd first thought.

Sophisticated people took just as dim a view of being caught as run-of-the-mill scum. At times, even more so.

He didn't release her until they reached his car. With a loud, indignant sigh, she rubbed her arm where his fingers had dug in. "I was beginning to think you were going to strap me to the roof."

He fixed her with a long, slow look that went way farther and deeper than he'd anticipated. Something stirred inside him, quickened in his belly, but he ignored it.

"The thought crossed my mind." Cade waited for her to get in first, then opened his own door. Getting in, he flipped on the headlights before starting the car. A soft-voiced tenor sang on the radio about the upside of heartache as Cade spared Mac a quick side glance. "You always been this single-minded?"

Since she had no choice at the moment, Mac sat back in her seat. "Pretty much."

It was the only way to get difficult things accomplished. Like becoming a dentist when her father initially had a completely different career picked out for her. He wanted her to be a teacher. A noble vocation, but one she had absolutely no aptitude for. He'd selected it purely because it was a traditional career for a woman, never once asking how she felt about it. But she'd let him know.

Mac briefly entertained the idea of keeping her own

counsel, but she was too agitated to be quiet for more than a few bars of the singer's song.

By the time they had left the lot, she launched into an explanation. "The way I figure it, Miss-Upstanding - Looking - Citizen - Slash - Kidnapper has enough of a lead on us already. I don't intend for her to get in another whole night as well."

Stopping at one of the three lights on the road to the John Wayne Airport, Cade looked at her. "Ever occur to you that this woman might sleep and eat like the rest of the world—barring you?"

If that was a put-down, Mac had heard far better ones aimed at her. She was the first to admit that she knew she rubbed some people the wrong way. But popularity wasn't her goal here.

"Then that'll put me ahead enough to catch up, won't it?"

Working his way down the road, Cade didn't bother commenting on her observation. It would only lead him into an argument, and he was beginning to entertain the healthy suspicion that people didn't win arguments against McKayla Dellaventura.

They also, he went on to discover less than ten minutes later, didn't stand much of a chance when she decided to turn on charm mixed liberally with heavy doses of vulnerability. She did both with aplomb and studied artistry.

Standing at the U.S. Airlines reservation desk now, Cade placed Randy's sketch in front of a young clerk.

"Were you on duty last night?" Mac asked the clerk before Cade could make the inquiry. He was getting more than a little irritated at being constantly usurped this way.

The man struggled to stifle a yawn as he straightened his jacket. "On duty every night, Tuesday through Saturday." Fingers poised on the keyboard, he looked from one to the other. "Where to?"

"Nowhere," Mac told him. "Just some information." She pressed on despite the disgruntled look on the clerk's face. "Did this woman book a flight to Phoenix last night? It's likely she paid in cash. Possibly traveling under the name of Susan Wiley." She rattled off all the information she had at her disposal.

Fully conscious and becoming every inch the company man, the clerk squared his shoulders. "I'm sorry, but I can't give out that sort of information."

Here we go again. Mac wasn't about to be dismissed. Digging into her purse, she continued laying a verbal siege to the clerk's fortress.

"She was traveling with a baby. An eighteen-month-old girl. Heather." Finding it, Mac placed the wallet-size photograph of her niece on top of the sketch. "She looks like this."

Curious, the clerk snuck a peek at the photograph, even while pretending not to. "Really, ma'am, I'm sorry, but I can't—"

Mac caught his hand, bringing his attention squarely to her face. "Please," she begged. "That's my daughter. She has my daughter."

As Cade watched, amazed and with growing admiration, Mac changed from what he was beginning to view as a human steamroller to a woman only the man behind the desk could help.

"She was kidnapped two days ago. Kidnapped during a traffic accident. The only witness said the kidnapper looked like this." Mac tapped the sketch intently. "My husband and I have been following the trail all day." She nodded toward Cade, leaving him temporarily speechless. "Please, you have to help me." The tears that spilled from her eyes landed on the man's hand as she grasped it.

Leery, nervous, moved by her plight and her tears, the clerk looked furtively to either side of him before he began keying something into the computer.

"I think I saw her," he allowed uneasily, his voice now low. "Going to Phoenix, you say?"

"That's what we think," Mac said eagerly. Without realizing it, she was now grasping Cade's hand, squeezing it as hard as she was hopeful. Her eyes never left the clerk.

Cade had the impression that she had stopped breathing as the man's fingers flew across the keys. The terminal was far from silent, but all either one of them heard were the clicking keys.

The clerk finally sighed as he pulled up the right screen. "Here, mother and child. Traveling to Phoenix. One way." He looked up, somewhat confused. "Says here her name is Lucy Carlyle."

That didn't surprise Cade. It was part of the cover. "Paid cash?"

A quick check provided the answer. The clerk nodded. "Yes."

"That's the one." Cocking his head, Cade leaned over the counter, trying to see the screen. "What time was the flight?"

Still trying to maintain some semblance of protocol, the clerk kept the screen facing him. "She took the seven-thirty flight out last night."

"Thank you." A sliver of emotion entered his

voice as Cade shook the clerk's hand. "Very much," he added.

"Hey, I hope you find her," the clerk called after them as they left the counter.

Looking over her shoulder, Mac flashed a smile in his direction. "Thanks, we will."

Cade heard the same fierceness in McKayla's voice as he had in her sister's hospital room. He didn't have to be told that McKayla didn't intend to give up until she recovered her niece. He was well acquainted with that sort of determination. And knew firsthand about the feeling that went with it.

A strange tingling sensation was traveling up his arm. His fingers, still captured in hers, he realized, were going numb.

"Not that I find the contact disturbing, but you can let go of my hand any time you decide you're up to it."

"What?" Mac stared vacantly at him before she realized that she was holding on to him. Embarrassed, she pulled her hand back. "Oh, sorry."

He flexed his fingers to get back the circulation. She wasn't as delicate-looking as her sister, but he hadn't expected her to have a grip like a vise. Cade nodded back at the clerk. "You played him as if he were a violin and you were a virtuoso. Where did you learn how to act like that?"

A half smile fluttered over her lips as his question unearthed a memory. "Under fire. Came in handy when my father would catch me sneaking in after curfew when I was a teenager."

Cade had a strong feeling that Mac had been more than a handful in those years, seeing as how she was turning out to be one now as well, for a completely different set of reasons. He stood back mentally and did a quick survey of the woman who had bomb-blasted her way into the middle of his life this morning. Beautiful in a natural, earthy sort of way, she exuded confidence in her every move. He found her independence an attractive quality, but not when it was running him over.

"So, now do you want to call it a night?" Even as he asked the question, he was fairly certain he knew what her answer would be.

Mac looked at him in surprise. "We're just getting started."

Cade had a feeling that she could fly to Phoenix right now on her own power. But that kind of energy had a habit of petering out at the worst time. "Shouldn't you call your husband?"

"Don't have one." Digging into her purse, she located her cell phone and pulled it out. "But I should call my brother, let him fill in Moira and my parents while you book us a flight." As she began to punch in Danny's number, Cade took the cell phone from her hand. Stunned, she looked at him. "What?"

He'd been patient long enough. But like a snowball traveling downhill, she was beginning to pick up speed, not to mention mass. If he wasn't careful, he was going to get plowed under unless he stopped her now.

Closing the phone, he handed it back to her. "Let's get a few things straight. If you're paying me to conduct an investigation, I'd appreciate it if you didn't keep trying to constantly take control." He saw anger crease her forehead, but continued talking. The last woman he'd been intimidated by had been Sister Michael. She'd been six feet tall, and he'd been eight years old. "If you want a sidekick, call someone else to join you. There's no need to pay me for my services, which, by the way, don't include tagging along."

It took her a minute to regroup. "Look, if I'm stepping on your toes or your feelings, I'm sorry, it's just that—"

"Feelings have nothing to do with it," he corrected her. "I understand what you're going through. I was there myself. *Am* there myself. But you can't just leap into this full throttle and keep going. If you don't refuel, your engine goes dry and you seize up."

She took exception to the analogy. "I'm a person, not a race car."

His hand remained on her arm, keeping her in place. "Same applies."

Mac had a feeling that he'd continue holding her until she gave in. Although she bristled at the idea, she temporarily relented. Blowing out a breath, she looked at him. "So what do you propose?"

Turning, Cade directed her toward the exit and the parking lot beyond. "We get some food. We look at what we've got. Call the detective in charge to find out if he has anything else—"

If the police had had anything to volunteer, they would have gotten in contact with someone in her family, who would have in turn called her. Her cell phone had remained silent. "But—"

Undaunted, Cade continued as they left the terminal "—or if we have anything for him. You work a lot better in this field if you don't butt heads."

The look she spared him could have sliced a tree in half. "I'm not interested in remaining in this field. I'm interested in finding my niece."

"Speaking of which, when did we become man and wife?"

"The second it played better that way." Stopping abruptly, Mac turned to confront him. "Look, I'm sorry I grabbed your hand back there, I'm sorry I stepped on your toes. I—"

He wasn't interested in getting or hearing apologies. That wasn't why he'd brought the matter up to begin with. She was beginning to look as if she were operating on the hairy edge. He didn't want to see her crash and burn and didn't have the time to take care of her if she did.

"How long since you've slept or eaten?"

The question took her aback. Mac dragged a hand through her hair. Maybe she did feel a little punchy, but there would be plenty of time to sleep later, when this was resolved.

"Since my father called me about Moira." Because Cade continued looking at her, she tried to pinpoint the time a little better—and failed. "Sometime day before yesterday. Evening, I guess." She looked at him. "I can sleep and eat on the plane."

"Not in that order," he said, dismissing her glibly. "I'm serious, McKayla. You want me on the case, you have to take a few orders. That's probably not anything someone like you is used to, but those are the rules." Finished, he waited for her answer.

Nobody called her McKayla except strangers and her parents. It always made Mac feel like squirming.

Just like the look in his eyes. Maybe the look in his eyes was a little more lethal, she decided.

She frowned, then threw up her hands. Like it or not, she needed him. That made him the one to call the shots. "Okay. I'll eat. Maybe sleep a few minutes if it makes you feel better." She shook her head, then allowed her expression to soften a little. "You're not as easygoing as you look."

With the reins of the investigation back in his hands, Cade unlocked the passenger door and held it open for her. "I won't ask if that's a compliment." And she wasn't volunteering an answer, he noticed. Watching her slide in, he shut the door for her. "There's a restaurant not too far from here," he informed her as he got in on his side.

Mac pulled on her seat belt, locking it into place. "Do I have to sit at the table until I clear my plate?"

He grinned at the implication, starting the car. "We'll play it by ear."

Mac hadn't realized she was hungry until she bit into the club sandwich. They had stopped at the family-style restaurant she'd pointed out to him just outside the airport. He'd obliged by giving her no argument about the choice. She just wanted to get the so-called feeding over with.

The stomach she'd been patently ignoring suddenly came to life, growling as the plate was set in front of her. Embarrassed, Mac looked at Cade.

"Don't say it," she warned.

His face was a mask of innocence. It didn't fool her for a minute. He was enjoying this. "Say what?"

"'I told you so.'" When he continued looking at

her, the soul of innocence, she bit back a flash of temper. Was he baiting her? "Don't tell me you didn't hear my stomach just now."

"Oakland probably heard your stomach," Cade commented dryly, watching the waitress set down his plate. He picked up his napkin. He would have chosen something fancier, something more in keeping with the woman he was with. But he knew the food here was good. All that mattered was getting something edible down. "But I never say 'I told you so.' You lose friends that way."

Mac doubted that he thought of her in that category. "How about clients?"

He took a sip of the soda he'd ordered before answering. "Hopefully, they only remain clients for a short amount of time before the case is resolved." He smiled at her. "In either case, I still don't like rubbing people's noses in their mistakes. That's not my idea of fun."

She had no idea why she wanted to ask him what was. But she shut the question away before it had a chance to advance to her tongue.

"That would make you an exceptional man, Cade." *A very exceptional man,* she caught herself thinking. Mac took another bite, nearly finishing her sandwich. "So, if I'm a very good girl and finish every last bit of my meal, then can we book the flight to Phoenix?"

Cade still thought it might be a better idea to fly out in the morning. He thought it was an even better idea if he could convince her to remain behind, but he knew he had as much chance of that as he did of stemming the tide during a hurricane. "There's someone I need to call first."

"The detective on the case?"

He shook his head. "You're only half right. I'm calling a detective I know. Kane Madigan. He has connections with the Phoenix police department. It never hurts to touch base with the police, especially in kidnapping cases."

Mac nodded. He was making sense. She supposed that she might be getting on his nerves, pushing the way she was. She briefly entertained the idea of apologizing to him, then let it go. He'd said he understood how she felt. That was enough. Apologies weren't easy for her.

She stared down into her soda, watching the last of the ice melt away in the glass. There was no explanation for why she felt this wave of loneliness overtake her. Mac looked up and saw that he was studying her.

"Do you think we'll find her? Your gut feeling," she added before he had a chance to reply.

She wasn't asking for his gut reaction, Cade thought. She was asking him to say yes. It was little enough he could do. "If we keep on going the way we have been, then yes, I think we'll find her."

"If?"

He wouldn't have been Cade if he wasn't somewhat honest with her. "There's always a chance we won't." He brushed that thought aside. "Right now, what I'm thinking is that this operation feels slick."

"Slick?"

"Well-thought-out," he elaborated. Cade drained the rest of his drink, then set it on the edge of the table. "The running-off-the-road failed," he pointed out, "so there was a contingency plan that went into effect almost immediately."

"If it was such a good plan, why did she need to call a cab? Why not just go off in her car?"

There was that, and it had bothered him somewhat. He shrugged. "Maybe car trouble. Maybe she felt she was being watched. Or maybe the car's a rental and she had to act fast. She doesn't care about the car, but she does about the baby."

"Heather." Mac didn't like the idea of Heather losing her identity and becoming just "the baby." There was something almost demoralizing about thinking of her in those terms.

Cade understood. "Heather," he corrected himself. "Something tells me that we're not dealing with a single kidnapping, but just one in a series of kidnappings."

Mac felt a cold chill shimmy up her spine. It surprised her that in the next moment, she found herself wanting him to put his arm around her to chase it away.

Chapter 6

"Phoenix?"

The single-word question followed her father's long pause on the other end of the line. Having finished with the meal Cade had insisted she eat, Mac had gone to the public telephones located between the restaurant's two rest rooms to call her family.

"That's where the trail seems to lead."

"Are you sure about this?"

With an inner sigh, Mac leaned against the wall and tried, for the most part, to avoid Cade's eyes.

Why did they have to be so dark, like a fathomless ocean at night? It was hard enough, holding her own against her father, when she was focused.

Holding the receiver in both hands, she tried to concentrate. "Sure that it leads to Phoenix? Yes. For now," she amended, not wanting to give her father anything to take her to task for later. "Maybe it goes farther, I don't know." She knew without asking what was on her father's mind. He wanted to be sure she didn't fail him. Not that she ever had, but he was the type who always anticipated the worst in every situation. "But don't worry, wherever it goes, I intend to follow it. So tell Moira and Mom not to worry. I'll bring Heather back with me." *Or I'm not coming back,* she added silently.

There was another pause before he spoke again. This time, his voice was not nearly as forceful as it usually was. "McKayla?"

She wondered if it was just her imagination that made him sound so uncertain. "Yes?"

There was a false start, followed by still another pause. And then the senior member of Dellaventura Dental, Inc., said, "Your mother and sister aren't the only ones who worry about you."

Was he going to chastise her for forgetting to mention her brothers in this? With her father, she never knew just when she stepped on toes, when she set him off. When she was younger, it had been a point of rebellion not to care, or to pretend that she didn't. But she was older now, and the games had long since ceased on her part. Her father was a good man, however gruff and devoid of demonstrative feelings, and she owed him her loyalty and respect. He had her love, too, although she really doubted that it mattered to him.

"I know," she concluded, "but Danny and Randy don't like to show it."

"That's not what I meant—that is—" Her father sounded annoyed. She was too tired to try to figure out why this time. "Just be careful, all right?"

The instruction, standing alone, caught her by surprise. "Is that an order?"

"No," he barked, then added a little more quietly, although not much, "it's a request."

Confused, she instinctively covered for him and the awkward moment that was born in the wake of his words. "Don't worry, Dad. Mrs. Jackson is bringing her triplets for their semi-annual checkup next week. I wouldn't miss that for the world." She heard her father grunt something almost unintelligible on the other end of the line. A mumbled good-bye was the last thing she heard before the connection was terminated.

"And good-bye to you," she murmured, hanging the receiver up.

Waiting by the hostess's desk, though close enough to see her, yet far enough to pretend to give her the privacy she might need, Cade straightened when he saw Mac hang up. He met her half way.

He couldn't quite read her expression. "What's wrong?"

Roused out of her thoughts, she looked up at him as if she'd temporarily forgotten he was there.

"Hmm? Oh, nothing. Nothing." But she could see by the look on Cade's face that he wasn't satisfied with her answer. She supposed she couldn't blame him. In his place, she wouldn't have been, either. Walking beside him, she forged ahead through the door rather than allow him to open it for her. "My father just told me he was worried about me. Not in so many words—words aren't his chosen method of communication—but in fragments and noises." Even as she said it, it seemed unreal.

Taking her literally, Cade smiled as he tried to imagine the exchange between father and daughter. Her father had struck him as a tough customer when he'd met him at the hospital.

"Must have made for an interesting conversation." He could see that she was serious. "Didn't he ever let you know he was worried about you before?"

"No." The response was so quick, it was almost automatic. Mac paused to reconsider, trying to be fair. But there wasn't a single time she could recall, even from her childhood, that her father had expressed concern about her.

"Worried that I wouldn't come through, maybe, but *about* me?" She shook her head. "No, never."

Cade hadn't been wrong in his assessment of her independent, controlling manner. She was accustomed not only to fending for herself, but in taking the helm in most matters. It was obvious that her father expected it of her, just as he expected her respect.

Maybe he was crazy, but he could have sworn he detected a trace of vulnerability in her again. "Well, like you said, he's not much on communication."

Preoccupied with her own interpretation of the conversation that had taken place, Mac looked at Cade. "What are you saying?" Mac asked.

Now that he was part of the club, he could well understand how other fathers felt. Other fathers who hadn't been born with the gift of being able to put their feelings into words.

"Only that most fathers worry about their kids whether they say it in so many words or not." The door closed behind him, and he stood on the wide stone step. "It's a given." As Mac watched, Cade's

regal-boned, almost-stoic face became animated.
There was a light in his eyes she could see even in
only the poor illumination from the lanterns along the
path leading up to the front entrance. "You watch
that tiny creation pop out into the world, take its first
breath, and suddenly nothing is ever the same again."
His eyes shifted away from his memories and he
looked at Mac. He supposed he was getting carried
away, but just this once, because it was Darin's birthday, because he missed him so much, Cade allowed
himself the moment's indulgence. "Everything is bigger, brighter—scarier."

"Scarier?"

Cade laughed softly to himself. It was a matter of
having to be part of the club before understanding
settled in.

"You start thinking in terms of how your child is
affected by things. Coffee tables suddenly have edges,
not just surfaces. Water glasses become shards of
glass waiting to happen." He enumerated just a frac-
tion of the things that had suddenly concerned him
when his son began walking. "The ground gets
harder, the distance between the bed and the floor
becomes a leap to be attempted only by an experienced stuntman." He stopped in the lot when he saw
the look on her face. "What?"

Mac had to laugh. "I just can't picture you worrying about things like that." He seemed too solid,
too much like a man who could see the forest because
the trees didn't get in his way. "Did you?"

"Not until my son was born," he admitted. And
then, much to his surprise and no little horror, it had
been a struggle not to get carried away. Elaine had

kept him grounded—until she'd died. And then he'd had to do it all alone.

Mac thought Cade was giving her father way too much credit. She supposed if she'd have to choose a father for her children, it would be someone like Cade, not someone like her own father, that she'd pick.

Not that there was much of a need for her to choose anyone, she thought ruefully. Not with the way her life was going these days.

"Must have been an adjustment for you," she commented as they reached his car.

Maybe he was saying too much. It was certainly a lot more than Cade had intended on sharing, but somehow, the words seemed to continue coming, nudged out by feelings he'd tried so hard to keep wrapped up. "One I didn't mind making."

Cade fished out his car keys. Mac looked at him, seeing him in a far different light than she had when she approached him for the first time. "How do you function with him—you know?" She couldn't make herself say it.

He shrugged. "You just do." He turned the key, unlocking her side. "You have to." Cade opened the door for her. "The alternative is to give up, and giving up is as good as saying he's gone." His jaw hardened, an outward sign of the rigid resolve that existed within. "My son is too full of life and energy to be gone."

There was something incredibly sexy about him at that moment. Human, and sensitive, and sexy. Mac wasn't sure just what possessed her, or even what happened, really. One second she was having a normal conversation about fathers with a father, the next, she was stretching up on her toes to brush her lips against his.

For the briefest of instants, the kiss threatened to flower, to grow into something far more, far different, than the initial contact had been intended. Cade took hold of her shoulders, bracing her, holding her, before he drew back his head, stunned at himself.

Pulling in a long, shallow breath, he looked at the woman he was holding. Belatedly, he remembered to drop his hands from her shoulders. Something small, elusive and warm was weaving through him, far too slippery to allow capture and examination.

After a beat, he found that his vocal cords were operational. "What was that for?"

Nervousness vibrated through Mac. Annoyed, she upbraided herself for allowing a completely stupid indulgence to take hold.

She cleared her throat. "For being a comfort. And for comfort." Feeling hopelessly self-conscious, something she strove never to allow herself to feel, Mac shoved her hands into her pockets and shrugged. She deliberately looked past his head as she spoke. "It just felt like something that needing doing." Her voice picked up speed as she floundered. "Chalk it up to being a little rattled, okay? I—"

"Mac?"

Her eyes darted to his face and away again; she was afraid she might see humor there at her expense. Her voice was guarded. "Yes?"

"It's okay," he said softly, fighting, he discovered, the very real urge to repeat what he deemed from her countenance she could only think of as a mistake. "I liked it."

"I didn't ask that." Mac only realized she'd snapped the words out after the fact. Annoyance at her own lack of control on so many levels grew.

Cade smiled. He'd had a tiny bit of insight into her when she kissed him; far more, he guessed, than she probably would have wanted him to.

"Yeah, you did," he assured her. Changing the subject before the indignation she felt compelled to display took her in deeper, he suggested, "Why don't I take you back to the office? You can pick up your car, drop it off at your place. Maybe even get a few hours' sleep." That would be the best thing for her. He knew the signs of exhaustion and she was there. "I'll pick you up in the morning. We'll go straight to the airport."

He made the last sound like a promise. But she didn't want promises, she wanted action. Immediate action. "But that means much more time that she—"

He anticipated her words. "The number she called in Phoenix belongs to a law firm," Cade reminded her patiently. Rounding the hood of the car, he got in on his side. She remained standing on her side, he noted. "We're probably not going to be able to find anything out in the middle of the night."

Giving in, at least for the duration of the debate, Mac got in. The more time that slipped by, the further away Heather felt. Mac could feel herself growing edgier. She yanked at the seat belt buckle, holding it suspended above the slot as she looked at him accusingly. "We might if we break in."

She'd seen too many detective thrillers, Cade thought. He started the car. "Only as a last resort."

All Mac could think of was Heather, being treated like some sort of commodity instead of a beautiful little girl. Her impatience got the better of her again.

"What are you, afraid of the illegality of the situation?" she demanded as he drove off the lot. "How legal is it to kidnap a helpless baby?"

She was asking questions she wouldn't have if she were thinking clearly. Which only underscored Cade's point. "You're getting punchy."

Mac didn't like her weaknesses pointed out. "No, I'm not." She twisted in her seat to look at him. "But I'd like to take a punch at someone."

Cade could see her doing it, too. Not that he really blamed her. "All in good time. But we need to get you home now."

"If I'm driving my car, I'll get myself home."

He intended to follow her and then remain in the vicinity for a while, just to assure himself that she wouldn't double back to the airport and take the next flight out to Phoenix.

"Just want to see where you live so I don't waste time traveling up and down little residential side streets, looking for your house early in the morning."

Why did Mac have the feeling that there was more to it than he was telling her? "I thought you were going to get in touch with someone about a Phoenix connection?"

He couldn't help smiling. She made it sound like something out of an action adventure movie about drug dealers. "And I intend to. But, unlike me, he has a life."

There was a time, when the tables had been turned. When he had been the one with a life and Detective Kane Madigan had been the one who lived and slept on the job. Home was just somewhere he received junk mail, a place that could have been described as a medium walk-in closet equipped with a refrigerator.

But now Kane had a wife and two children and an extended family. People who allowed him to fully exercise that muscle Cade had always believed his friend had—a heart. And now he was the one who had no life beyond his work, no interests beyond the cases he took and the one case that pressed so heavily on his own heart.

"You think you might be up against a baby-selling ring?" Kane asked.

"It's crossed my mind," Cade admitted as he proceeded to touch on the case's key points. Cade also relayed the details his contact on the Newport Beach police force had told him. Apparently, the police had uncovered an abandoned dark blue Camry that suspiciously matched the description the first set of bickering paramedics had given.

Kane made a few notes to himself. Running down kidnappers had become his personal crusade since he had found Jennifer's baby and he'd married the single mom. "You might have something there. Ours was taken by a woman posing as a nurse. Came in to take the baby for a test and then disappeared off the face of the earth. Until we found her."

Cade could only hope that the resolution in Heather's case would turn out as well. "I love a happy ending."

Kane thought of the little girl he'd adopted. He couldn't love her more than if she were his own. "Yeah, me, too. You'll want to contact Lieutenant Graham Redhawk. Great guy." With precise, efficient words he told Cade what he knew about the Phoenix detective. "He was there for us when I was trying to track down Jennifer's little girl. I'll give him a call to let him know you're on your way and I'll keep good thoughts for you about this."

"Thanks."

Kane knew that the other man was about to hang up. Part of him was tempted to let him without asking, but that was the coward's way out. He'd never been accused of that and didn't intend to begin now. "And Cade?"

"Yeah?"

"No word about your boy?"

"None." The word felt as if it had been wrenched out of his gut as he said it. Cade thought of the updated photograph Megan had fed into the Web site that dealt with missing and abused children before she'd left the office again. How many more updates would there be before he held his son in his arms again? "It's late, I'd better go. Thanks again for your help."

Cade had his complete sympathy. Kane didn't know how he would have withstood not knowing where either of his daughters were for the space of a few hours, much less three years. "Don't mention it. Let me know what happens, okay?"

At times, faced with nothing but night and his own thoughts, it was hard for Cade to keep his grasp on a positive outlook. But he had no choice. The alternative, if he allowed it through, would kill him.

So he infused his positive attitude into his voice and promised, "Sure thing."

No matter how many times she tossed and turned, searching for that one elusive spot where sleep and oblivion dwelled, Mac couldn't find it. She couldn't sleep. Like a child's top, she was wound up so tightly Mac was certain she'd spin forever if someone released her.

This wasn't any good.

Damn, she should have insisted on getting the red-eye instead of agreeing to this, she thought, punching her pillow.

Defeat circling her, Mac sat up. Dragging a hand through her tousled hair, she looked down at her bed. With tangled sheets and a blanket that was nearly in a knot, it looked as if a battle had been fought there.

And maybe there had been, she thought groggily. A battle with her emotions.

Mac pulled her knees up to her chest. She wasn't going to get any real rest until she found her niece.

"Damn it, why did this have to happen?"

The question ricocheted around the small bedroom, moving from space to space unanswered.

It didn't matter why, she told herself, what mattered was that it had. What mattered more was getting Heather back.

But that wasn't the only thing keeping her up, although it was more than enough.

There was something else. Something small and insignificant, but disconcerting for all that. Something that kept her awake just like the tiny pea had kept the princess awake in that long-forgotten fairy tale she could remember reading to Moira when she was five and her sister was three.

A small, sad smile curved her lips. There wasn't a time in her life when she hadn't felt responsible for Moira. For all of them, she amended silently, to a greater or lesser degree. That included her gruff father. Her life had always been so hectic, so full...

That was why...why she'd been so surprised when she'd kissed Cade. Maybe even more surprised than he was, but not by much.

What had possessed her?

It was that look in his eyes, she rationalized. The look that reached out to her, bridging across the fact that for all intents and purposes, they were strangers, that their only relationship was that of client and investigator.

She had acted instead of thought.

She hadn't sifted through it the way she was doing now. What she had done was gone with a feeling. A need. A bonding.

Who knew, maybe she needed to kiss him more than he needed to be kissed by her? Mac thought as she threw herself down on the bed and tried to sleep again.

The knock, louder now and forceful, burrowed its way through layers of heavy fog, breaking ground in Mac's brain and clearing a path with persistence.

Knocking.

Someone was knocking. On her door.

With a gasp of surprise, she bolted upright as the

realization that she was sleeping suddenly burst on her brain. Not just sleeping. Oversleeping.

She glanced frantically at her clock even as she hit the ground, moving. It was eight. The flight to Phoenix she'd made Cade book last night was leaving in an hour and five minutes.

And she was practically brain dead, rushing for the door.

She was also naked as the day she was born. Horror ricocheted through her as she saw her reflection in a mirror.

How could she have forgotten she slept in the nude?

With a squeal, she grabbed the huge crochet throw on the sofa that her sister had made for her, pausing only long enough to wrap it around herself before continuing on.

From the other side of the door, Cade heard the squeal. He was already concerned that she hadn't instantly answered the doorbell when he'd rung it. He'd arrived, half expecting her to be standing on her doorstep, waiting for him.

"McKayla, is everything all right?" he called through the door.

"I'm coming," she yelled.

Annoyed with herself, she fumbled with the locks with one hand as she held on to the sinking crocheted throw with the other. With a heavy sigh, she yanked open the door and stumbled back, admitting him in.

"I thought something was...wrong."

Cade stopped as he turned to look at her. The look quickly transformed into a stare. The wrap she was clutching to her was yellow and white, dipping down low behind her and drooping off to one side. It also left little to the imagination, laying open a great many spaces for a libido to leap in, even one as dormant as his.

There was no doubt about it. The yellow daisies were not as tightly crocheted as they might have been, and the squares they were nestled in were not as well-joined as the original pattern undoubtedly had called for. The result was that it displayed more than it hid and instantly called a dormant imagination back to active duty.

Seeing her like this reminded Cade of something that he'd forgotten. That he wasn't just an investigator, but a man as well. A man who hadn't been with a woman in a very long time.

Chapter 7

"Don't you think that's a little chilly for Phoenix this time of year?" Cade finally asked.

The right thing to do was to ignore the fact that she was apparently underdressed even for skiing in the Alps, but he couldn't quite get himself to do it. Any more than he could resist letting his eyes sweep over her just once.

And linger.

He'd had no idea that her figure was quite that spectacular.

Though Mac tried valiantly to ignore it, embarrassment was taking a healthy chunk out of her. Feeling uncustomarily shaken, she flashed him a smile, attempting to gloss over her predicament.

"I overslept." Pivoting on her heel, she hurried back into the bedroom. "Couldn't sleep until probably ten minutes ago," she called out as she disappeared into the other room.

He resisted the urge to follow her. "Still doesn't explain the unusual ensemble."

"I sleep in the nude."

Her explanation exploded into his thoughts, sending them in a whole new direction while leaving his tongue behind. But that was because he'd almost swallowed it. The images her explanation raised also raised his temperature several degrees higher than he was comfortable with.

Very slowly, he blew out a breath, telling himself that a man his age had no business reacting that way.

The lecture didn't help.

"That would explain it," he remarked. Given that she hadn't answered her bell the first two times he'd rung and had hastily donned the teasing throw, Cade figured he'd obviously woken her up. He glanced at his wristwatch. There was no way they were going to get to the airport in time.

"Um, look—" Cade raised his voice even more, not sure how far it would have to carry "—I can try to rebook the flight."

"No!" Hand holding on to the doorjamb, Mac poked her head out of the room to underscore the command. Cade had the feeling that all she was wearing at the moment was her expression. He could feel his gut tightening a notch more, almost cutting off his air supply entirely. "I can get ready in time."

He sincerely doubted it, but debating the issue would only steal precious time away, so he said nothing.

Feeling at loose ends and needing something to keep his hands occupied with, if not his mind, he looked around the room. It was a cozy house, he thought, if the room he was in was any indication what the rest of it looked like. She obviously wasn't obsessive about keeping things neat. Elaine had been. He'd no sooner put a newspaper down than it was refolded and whisked away, deposited in the recycle stack. A little bit of clutter was comfortable, made a place looked lived in, but his wife had had different views on that.

He supposed his approval of Mac's housekeeping methods was just thinly disguised rationalization of his own haphazard methods. He wasn't very big on cleaning. But to his credit, he didn't make that much of a mess, either.

He could see the kitchen off to the left. He figured it was a safe bet that she hadn't eaten yet.

Taking a step in the direction of the kitchen, he stopped, not wanting to get ahead of himself here. She might think he had another destination and something entirely different in mind.

Shoving his hands into his back pockets, he asked, "Anything you want me to do to help you get ready?"

There was a pause from the other room, as if she was trying to follow him. "You mean, like pull up my zipper?"

He had no intention of getting that close to her, at least not for the time being. The less physical contact he had with her right now, Cade decided, the clearer he could keep his head.

He crossed to the telephone instead, positive they had to cancel their tickets and reschedule the flight. That would give him enough time to catch up with

Megan and see if she had anything on the leads he'd asked her to follow up on.

Cade looked around, wondering where she kept her white pages. "No, I was thinking more along the lines of making you a fried egg sandwich."

"You can do that?"

He blinked. The white pages were forgotten. Mac was walking out of her bedroom, slipping on a second dangling earring. There was a pair of shoes, navy to match her suede skirt, tucked under her arm. Barring the two items, she was completely dressed. If she'd hurried into her clothes, she certainly didn't give that impression.

"Yeah," he said, remembering to answer, though the word dribbled out of his mouth as he stared at her in amazement. "Fried egg sandwiches are my specialty. How did you do that?"

"Do what?"

Sidestepping her coffee table and the telephone, he crossed to her. She looked like the up-and-coming executive of some pricey company. He'd expected her to come out wearing jeans and a sweatshirt.

Despite what she was wearing, he couldn't get the image of Mac and the slipping crocheted throw out of his mind.

They were talking, he suddenly remembered. And it was his turn. Struggling, he focused. "Get dressed so fast." Her explanation about acting came back to him. "Or is that something else you learned to do to avoid your father's suspicions?"

Halfway to the front door, Mac stopped and turned to him. She had no idea why, but she fluttered her eyelashes at Cade, murmuring, "Why, Mr. Townsend, what kind of a girl do you take me for?'' in her best Tennessee Williams wanton-heroine voice.

For the second time in the span of less than ten minutes, Cade found himself robbed of the ability to form coherent words. Collecting himself, he attempted a graceful retreat. Even as he opened his mouth, he knew he was doomed to go the graceless way.

"Sorry, didn't mean to imply…that is, it's none of my business.…'' He tried again, pouncing on the only thing that appeared to be a given. "Are you ready to go, then?"

She was flattered, Mac realized. In the middle of a highly charged, emotional situation that demanded her full attention, she was flattered. Flattered by the attention of a man who she'd wager didn't spread his attention liberally.

Not the time, or the place, she told herself.

The feeling didn't leave immediately.

Grabbing her purse and picking up the small travel bag she'd thrown together last night, Mac announced, "Yes," and then made it to the front door before Cade did.

"Don't you want to lock the front door?" he called after her.

She turned, but remained where she was. "It's self-locking. Let's go." She made a beeline for his car.

She had to wait for him to unlock the door. Sliding into the passenger seat, Mac let out her first long breath, trying to calm down a little. She disliked flying, and boarding the plane feeling this way wasn't the best idea.

It had been a challenge, getting ready so fast. She

couldn't remember ever having gotten completely dressed in under five minutes before, not even on the mornings she'd overslept during her days at the dorm.

But then, there was a lot more at stake here than just a good grade or maintaining a stellar GPA for the sake of her own pride. And because she'd wanted to prove herself to her father.

Mac turned to look at Cade as he started the car. He looked a little like she felt. Mac couldn't help wondering why.

"You look a little dazed around the edges." Was there something he wasn't telling her? "Anything wrong?"

Taking a shortcut out of the development, he bypassed the main thoroughfare. This time in the morning, it was sure to be snarled. The key word *through* didn't apply.

"No, I just never knew that hurricanes could assume human form." He spared her a glance before turning his attention back to the traffic. "Most people take longer to sign their name on a check than it took you to get ready."

She shrugged. It would have been nice to have gotten a shower in, but that was the price she paid for the kind of night she'd had. "I didn't want to miss the flight."

Even the best of intentions could only speed a person up so much, Cade thought. The fact that she could get ready faster than the average person took to drink a cup of coffee put her in a class by herself.

He had no idea why the thought of her moving fast seemed to naturally hook up to his wondering what she was like in bed. If making love with her was like trying to catch the wind in his hands. Or like being sucked into the middle of a Missouri twister, circling around in its funnel.

Not that the question—or its hypothetical answer—had any bearing on anything, least of all the case, he reminded himself.

He kept his eyes on the road and tried to keep his mind on avoiding the traffic in order to reach the airport in time.

"Did you call your friend?"

The question severed his concentration in half. "Hmm?"

"Your friend—the man you thought might connect you to someone in Phoenix—" she prompted. She couldn't remember whether or not he'd mentioned a name.

A glance from him had the color rising along her neck again. Mac didn't have to look in the mirror to know it was there, she could feel it. It was almost as if she could read his mind. He probably thought she was some sort of eccentric, answering the door wearing something that belonged on the back of a sofa.

Coming to a stop at a red light, Cade looked at her. Watching the color creep up almost made him forget his answer. He'd never thought of a blush as captivating before. Hadn't even thought someone as vital as McKayla was even capable of blushing. It was obvious that she wasn't quite as brash and pushy as she wanted people to believe she was.

"Oh, yeah. I called Kane. He gave me the name of a Lieutenant Graham Redhawk."

She nodded. "He'll be able to help us?"

Cade gave her only the facts, not wanting to mislead her with false information or hopes. "Well, he did when Kane was tracking down a black-market baby ring." He recalled the newspaper story. Kane had headed up the task force after a rash of kidnappings had broken out between here and Phoenix. But this situation wasn't exactly the same.

Black-market baby ring. Mac hated the way that sounded, but each time the subject was raised, it became more of a viable possibility to her.

"Is that who you think took Heather?" Her lips dry, she slid her tongue across them unconsciously. "A professional kidnapping ring?"

"Not the same group…" Cade began to point out, but then, now that he thought of it, who knew? Just because one head of the monster had been struck off didn't mean that another one hadn't grown in its place, or sprung up somewhere else, for that matter. "But it's a strong possibility." He saw a parking space and went for it. The airport lot was too full to pick and chose. "We need to keep an open mind on this."

"Open, closed, I don't care," Mac told him, trying to curb impatience that periodically flashed within her like an unexpected frying pan fire. "All I want is Heather back."

Cade pulled up the hand brake with a jerk. "We'll get her back," he promised.

Mac wanted to ask how he could sound so sure, but if she did, she was afraid that the fragile bubble that she'd surrounded herself with would burst.

Getting out of the car, Mac shook her head. She would have never thought she was the type to need nebulous assurances, the type who was willing to take up residence in a castle in the sky without carefully checking the foundations. But in this case, she'd moved in, lock, stock and barrel, without so much as a cursory glance at the underpinnings. Deliberately avoiding so much as a look in their direction. All she required from Cade was periodic reaffirmation of the same vague statement he'd just given her.

She clung to it like a security blanket. Until there was more to go on, it was all she had.

"I'll hold you to that," she murmured as they raced for the proper gate.

"Anything?" Balancing a cardboard tray containing food from a nearby take-out place, Cade asked the question as he nodded toward the door on the driver's side of the car he'd rented at the airport three hours ago.

Mac leaned over and opened the door for him, then sat up again. Sitting down, Cade precariously placed the tray between them.

His legs protested as he took up his post again. They had been sitting here, across the street from the law office of Phillip Taylor, the man the kidnapper had called from her Bedford hotel room, for the last three hours. They had come here straight from the airport, partially on Mac's insistence.

From the looks of it, they were destined to maintain their vigil for another three hours, if not more.

"No," Mac answered with a sigh. "Nothing."

Though she'd agreed when he offered to get her something, Mac wasn't particularly moved by the thought of eating anything. Her stomach was too tied up in knots. She deposited the yellow-wrapped offering Cade had just handed her on the dashboard, satisfying herself with a sip of the soda.

Her eyes ached from staring at the doorway. People had come and gone all day, but none of them bore even a faint resemblance to the woman in the sketch.

Normally, Cade enjoyed Mexican food, even the junk-food kind. But this time he ate without tasting, his attention cornered by the woman beside him. She was fidgeting, even though she wasn't actually moving. He could feel it.

Finishing the enchilada, he balled up the paper. "You don't do waiting very well, do you?"

She laughed softly under her breath. "Does it show?"

Despite the soft music coming from the radio he'd left on, tension filled the interior of the car. "Only in a really big way. Other than that, no."

Mac looked at him, searching his face for telltale signs she'd become accustomed to seeing on other people. "Am I getting on your nerves yet?"

"No, why? Is there a time limit on that?"

She shrugged carelessly, thinking that maybe she shouldn't have said anything. It was just that she didn't want to get on his nerves. So far, he'd been very accommodating. She didn't want to repay him by being a pain. If there was more to it than that, she wasn't willing to explore it.

"No, it's just that I have my own way of doing things—" She looked away. She was better off watching the small office building, she thought, than letting her mind wander.

Cade laughed. There was that gift for understatement again. "I noticed." He stuffed the yellow paper into the empty bag, thinking that maybe he should have gotten two orders for himself. Breakfast seemed a long way away.

"Yes, so do most people, and it gets on their nerves. I was just wondering if I had gotten on yours yet."

"No, not yet. I'll let you know when." She flinched, her eyes darting to him, when his cell phone rang. She made him think of a powder keg, about to take off. "Relax, it's probably just Megan."

At least, he hoped it was Megan. With any luck, she was calling with a little positive feedback. He could use some about now, as well as something to take his mind off the fact that he was sharing a very small space with a very vibrant woman.

"You're expecting her call?" Mac asked, running her hand along the back of her neck.

"Yes. I called her earlier, asking her to run some things down for me."

He'd left the message on Megan's answering machine in the office, hoping to catch her at some point, preferably early in the day. They each contributed something different to ChildFinders. Sam brought his multitude of connections, and Megan brought her considerable computer expertise. While he, Cade supposed, was the heart of the organization. He liked to think he was what drove it toward its excellent track record.

"Hello?"

Glancing at him again, Mac could tell from the easy smile sliding over his lips that he'd been right in his guess. It was Megan. Mac had trouble drawing her eyes away from his smile. It was warm and incredibly comforting. She didn't begin to speculate why. That was better left untouched.

So instead, she watched the stucco-and-wood building across the street and listened to Cade.

"You can? Megan, you're a doll. I owe you one. Okay, three," he amended.

The note of easy camaraderie caught her ear, making her feel somewhat envious. What did it feel like, being that comfortable with someone? Was there someone in his life he was completely at home with? Had that been why he'd backed off when she'd kissed him yesterday? Because he felt loyalty to another woman?

He was the type, she thought. Like a swan, or an elephant, Cade Townsend struck her as the type of person who committed himself for life to a single soul mate.

She was being hopelessly romantic. Or hopelessly naive, she thought, upbraiding herself.

Turning in her seat, she pounced on him the second he broke off the connection. Mac knew without being told that whatever had gone on between them had to do with Heather. "What did she say?"

Instead of answering her immediately, Cade got out of the car and opened the rear passenger door. As she twisted in her seat to watch, he got into the back seat and opened up the briefcase he'd brought on the plane with him. He took out a notebook computer and the smallest printer she had ever seen. Moving with practiced speed, Cade hooked up the printer to his cell phone.

He still hadn't answered her. "Are you setting up an office back there?"

He glanced at the back seat. He was perched on the edge to make room for the electronic hardware.

"Something like that. Megan got in contact with someone she knew from the bureau—" he glanced up "—Megan used to be a special agent with the FBI. They found some prints in the ambulance."

She held her breath, not sure where this was going, only that it had to help. "And?"

He knew this was going to disappoint her. Double-checking, he read the screen. "No criminal record, but there was a fairly clear thumbprint she managed to check out with the DMV. At least we have a name. And a real photograph." Which, in the long run, was more important than a name the woman could change whenever the whim hit her.

As he filled Mac in, the printer suddenly came to life, making far more noise than its size would have warranted. Within moments, they had a somewhat blurred reproduction of a driver's license photograph.

Holding it aloft, he said to Mac, "Meet Shirley Lambert." He leaned forward, offering the photograph to her as his printer began working on a second page. "That may or may not be her real name, but at least it was when she got this license. It's expired now, but Megan used her social security number from her file to trace her to Phoenix, where she seems to be currently living. At least it gives us somewhere to start."

Closing everything up again, he got out and returned to the front seat.

Mac stared at the photograph. Shaking her head, she handed the photograph back to him.

"The paramedics were right. If this woman ap-

proached me, I wouldn't have thought twice, either.
She looks like the soul of propriety.'' She paused,
pressing her lips together. ''You're right, you know.
This has the feeling of being bigger than just
Heather's kidnapping.''

''The question is, how big.'' He paused, looking
over the second sheet that Megan had just forwarded
to him. This one was on the lawyer's background. It
looked impressive. ''The lawyer Shirley's mixed up
with specializes in private adoptions.'' Cade skimmed
over the numbers Megan had compiled for him. So
many lives affected by this man. Folding the sheet,
he tucked it into his pocket. ''You can't help wondering how many of those adoptions involve kids
whose parents are still looking for them.''

The implication behind his question was too vast,
too horrible for Mac to contemplate. It was bad
enough just thinking about Heather's abduction. And
then a thought hit her.

''But if *we* think that, why haven't the police come
across them before?''

It was a good question, but Cade had no answers.
''Maybe there hasn't been anything to tie them to a
kidnapping before. These people aren't amateurs.''
That was clear from the lawyer's apparent standing.
''Most of the adoptions are probably aboveboard.''
He considered the situation, trying to put himself in
the lawyer's shoes. ''But maybe the supply dries up
every so often, and Taylor and his little band have
been helping it along just enough to keep it moving.''
He sighed, looking toward the building. ''There's no
telling how long it might have been going on.''

''So what do we do now?''

"We stay here a little longer to see if our lady friend shows up." He knew she didn't like that. But if the woman showed up, there might be a strong chance that she could lead them back to Heather, or at least to the next step in finding her. "If not, we check out her address." He had a feeling it was bogus. "And we have a conversation with Lieutenant Graham Redhawk."

It sounded like a great deal of wheel-spinning to her. "And that's all?"

There was something else Cade was working on in the back of his mind, something that was a little bit more intricate than what he'd just proposed to her. But he didn't want to talk about it until it was time. "No, but it's a start."

Mac shifted in her seat. Frowning, she sighed. "I guess walking in and beating the information out of him is out of the question?"

He laughed. "That's the backup plan." The woman certainly could never be accused of being passive. And somehow Cade found that very appealing.

Chapter 8

"**K**ane called and told me you might be stopping by," Lieutenant Graham Redhawk said as he ushered Mac and Cade into an empty office.

"I'm Dr. McKayla Dellaventura. Heather's my niece." She was getting ahead of herself again, Mac thought. "Did Kane also tell you what this was about?"

Gray nodded. "Dirty business," he agreed heartily without waiting for the sentiment to be expressed aloud. "How can I help you?"

"Officially?" Mac wanted to be perfectly clear about just what sort of help they could expect, if any. In her experience, anything official came wrapped up in miles of sticky, impeding red tape.

"Officially or unofficially, makes no difference as long as laws aren't broken outright." He studied their faces and satisfied himself as to their involvement.

"Can't think of anything worse than having your child stolen from you. No matter what the age," he tagged on.

Gray's first was growing so fast these days, it was hard remembering what the boy had been like at Heather's age.

"How can I help?" he repeated more softly, this time looking at Mac.

Very quickly, Cade filled Gray in on the events of the last two days, giving him all the information they had at their disposal.

Fishing out the DMV photograph that Megan had faxed to him earlier, Cade placed it on the desk next to Gray's thigh. "We think the kidnapper is this woman."

Gray picked up the rendition and carefully studied the face in the photograph. Neither the name nor the face rang any bells. "I can run her for a list of priors."

"She hasn't any," Cade told him. "At least, not under that name."

Gray opened the door. "No offense, but I like checking things out for myself." Sometimes two sets of eyes help. "Maybe there's something in our program that isn't in yours." He began walking out toward the receptionist. "Gretchen, would you mind running this through the system? I need this in a hurry," he told her as the woman took the sheet.

Graham was back in the captain's office, about to close the door when Gretchen actually looked down at the photograph. "Why are you running Mrs. Lambert through the system?"

Mac was on her feet instantly, crossing to the

younger woman before Gray had a chance to say anything. She grasped Gretchen by the shoulder, unconsciously afraid that this newest connection was just a product of her overly tired brain. "You *know* her?"

"Well, yeah." Pausing, Gretchen looked back down at the photograph to make sure she hadn't made a mistake. "She's my doctor's nurse. His wife, actually. Her name's Shirley Lambert, just like the license says."

Mac was less interested in the validity of the name than she was in what Gretchen had just said. "Doctor? What kind of doctor?"

She stared at Mac with just a touch of apprehension. "An ob-gyn, why?" The receptionist looked from the woman to the other man and then finally at Gray. "Is something wrong?"

Mac's heart was hammering hard enough to leave dents in her rib cage. She looked at Cade. "Are you thinking what I'm thinking?"

Cade nodded. "I am if you're thinking it's a perfect tie-in."

He knew Mac had been concerned about Heather's condition because of the accident. For the kidnapper to go to a doctor would have been difficult, arousing suspicions not easily fielded. There would be questions to answer and forms to fill out—unless there was a doctor in the organization, ready to treat any problem that came up.

This bore further examination, Gray thought. "Gretchen, would you mind joining us for a minute?" Motioning to a chair, Gray waited for the receptionist to sit down.

Gretchen bit an overly red lower lip. "The captain wants me to run a check on—"

"The captain won't be back until tomorrow morning. This will only take a minute," Gray assured her. When she sat down hesitantly, he closed the office door. "Relax," he counseled. "I just need a little information. Does your doctor have any areas of specialization, beside being an ob-gyn?"

It was obvious to all three of them that Gretchen was uncomfortable with the question. She stared for a long time at a stain in the carpet. "Infertility. My husband and I wanted a large family—someday." She directed her words at Mac, as if it was easier to talk to her than it was to Gray. "But by the time I was ready, 'someday' seemed to have moved on. Someone told me that Dr. Lambert practically guaranteed you a baby." Her voice picked up a little volume as she continued. "He does a whole battery of tests, works up a profile, and then if everything he tries fails, he offers other types of assistance."

"Other types?" Gray prodded.

She took a deep breath. "Fertilization outside the mother. That's the stage Tim and I are at now." It was obvious from her expression that she didn't want to go into any greater detail.

It wasn't exactly what he was hoping to hear. Cade placed a hand on her shoulder, drawing her attention. "Do you know if he sometimes offers to help couples with private adoption arrangements?"

"I wouldn't know." She looked at Gray. "Is that all? I've got to get back—"

"Sure." He opened the door for her. "Thanks for your time."

Almost out of the office, Gretchen suddenly turned around. Her brow was puckered as if she was trying to clarify a memory more clearly.

"You know, now that you mention it, I do remember overhearing a conversation in the waiting room once." Her eyes darted back and forth, unseeing, as she stared into the past. "Something about the doctor helping this woman find her a baby." A flush of triumph colored her cheeks as she looked at Gray. "'Connection with an angel,' she called it."

Mac latched onto the one word that jumped out at her. *"Find."* She was at Gretchen's side, turning her toward her. "You're sure she used the word *find?"*

Gretchen chewed into her lipstick a little further, eating away the red hue. Some of the hesitant air faded. "Pretty sure." Her dark eyes shifted back to Gray. "What's this all about?"

"I'm not sure yet," Gray told her honestly. It was best if she remained in the dark as much as possible if Lambert proved to be part of the ring. A rather ugly picture had begun forming in his head. "But add Dr. Lambert to your search for priors. And don't say anything to anyone."

Looking skeptical, Gretchen hurried from the room.

Cade waited until Gray closed the door again. "This Dr. Lambert, is there any way to find out if he has any priors anywhere in the country? Specifically if he had his license revoked in any other state." An embittered man might find a special sort of revenge in living well after suffering that sort of humiliation, Cade thought.

"That sort of information isn't readily available.

Like any other fraternal group, the AMA protects its own."

"You'd need a hacker," Mac interjected. "Given that the information exists in some database."

Cade thought of Sam's wife. If Megan couldn't be reached, he'd place a call to Savannah. She had the ability to make computers do anything short of assuming a secret identity. And there was the added bonus of Savannah having been in exactly the same situation that Mac's sister now found herself in. "I have access to a very good hacker," Cade told her.

Gray held up his hands. "I didn't hear that." His voice dropped. "Call whoever you have to. In the meantime, Gretchen'll try to see if there's anything readily available on Lambert."

"You could try passing his thumbprint through the system," Mac suddenly suggested.

He looked at her. "You have his thumbprint?"

"No, but the California DMV might. Since his wife had a license from there as Shirley Lambert, there's every reason to suspect the good doctor's originally from there, too," Mac speculated.

It was something to start with for now. Nodding, Gray opened the door. A wall of noise immediately pushed its way in. He raised his voice. "Wait here and let me tell Gretchen."

Excitement coursed through Mac's body. She felt as if she were going to leap out of her skin. The true irony of the saying "so near and yet so far" hit home. They'd gotten farther than she'd hoped, but not nearly as far as she would have liked.

Unable to sit, she paced around the small room, stopping by the window. She was out there somewhere, her niece. One small, helpless being in a city of—how many? Too many, Mac thought with a frustrated sigh.

She nearly jumped when she felt a hand on her shoulder. Swallowing the yelp that rose in her throat, she swung around to find herself looking up into Cade's eyes. Eyes like the warm waves of the Mediterranean Sea.

"We're making progress." Low, soft, soothing, his voice would have been infinitely comforting under normal circumstances. For now, she appreciated the gesture and the thought that was behind it.

"I know," she answered. "But not fast enough. If this is a black market, if these people are dealing with stolen babies, then Heather could be anywhere by now." She struggled not to let that thought choke the very air out of her lungs.

"That police detective I called, Kane Madigan," Cade began, "had his stepdaughter abducted straight out of a hospital. She'd already been placed in a home when they broke up the ring." Without realizing it, he took her hands in his. They were icy. He clasped his hands around them, trying to warm them. "But Kane and his wife managed to track her down—with Redhawk's help." His eyes held hers. He was talking now to the fears that were threatening to engulf her, trying to help her hold them at bay. "It'll be all right."

It was a promise, Mac realized. A promise Cade meant to keep no matter what. There was no real, logical reason to believe that he could actually deliver. It wasn't up to him, not in the long run.

And yet, she believed him. With her whole heart

and soul. The comfort she derived from the very sound of his voice amazed her.

"Did I just hear my name being mentioned?" Walking in, Gray pretended not to notice that he had interrupted something.

Cade released Mac's hands, stepping away from her and toward the police detective. "Just singing the praises that Kane sang to me about you."

Gray laughed under his breath. The sound was amazingly soft, given the demeanor of the man. "Well, I won't say that Kane tends to exaggerate, because the man hardly talks unless prodded. But if there's credit to be taken, it mainly belongs to him. The only thing I can tell you until Gretchen finishes her search is that there hasn't been a rash of infant kidnappings here or in any of the surrounding areas." He'd checked that out himself after talking to Kane. "There have been a couple of abductions, but nothing to lead us to believe that it was an ongoing issue."

It was beginning to get to her. She thought of the Web site Cade had shown her at his office yesterday afternoon. The one that was bursting at the seams with statistics on missing children.

"Just your run-of-the-mill, ordinary kidnappings." The bitterness in her own voice pulled her up short. She flashed an apologetic look in Gray's direction. "I'm sorry. I'm afraid I'm getting a little edgy."

"She's had five minutes' sleep, spread over two days," Cade explained to Gray.

Mac was surprised not to feel the customary flash of temper she usually experienced when someone apologized for her. She had no idea why, but hearing Cade make the excuse on her behalf made her feel as if they were a unit, something closer than just two people thrown together by circumstances for a short duration.

Maybe she was just getting punchy again. But whatever the reason, something warm struggled to open within her.

"Been there myself," Gray concurred, dismissing the incident as if it never existed. "You'll sleep when this is over, right?" he asked her.

It was Cade who answered again. "She'd better sleep soon, or we're all in a lot of trouble."

Mac started to ask him just what he meant by that, but Gretchen picked that moment to knock, poking her head in. "Sorry, nothing on Lambert or his wife."

"I can take a run up to their house," Gray volunteered, but without enthusiasm. "But if these people are as sharp as we think they are, I doubt if your niece is there."

Maybe it was the lack of sleep, or the situation, or a combination of everything, but her mind had been scrambling, linking fragments of thoughts together ever since Gretchen had mentioned seeing the doctor herself. Mac looked at Gray suddenly, only half realizing that he was talking.

"Why don't I go?"

Both men looked at her. "To the house?" Gray asked.

"No." Trying her best to be coherent, she waved away his question. "To the doctor. To Lambert," she stressed in case they weren't following her. "Gretchen said he specializes in infertility. Why don't I tell him that I've been trying unsuccessfully to get pregnant for several years now, and—"

GET A FREE TEDDY BEAR...

You'll love this plush, cuddly Teddy Bear, an adorable accessory for your dressing table, bookcase or desk. Measuring 5 ½" tall, he's soft and brown and has a bright red ribbon around his neck – he's completely captivating! And he's yours *absolutely free*, when you accept this no-risk offer!

AND TWO FREE BOOKS!

Here's a chance to get **two free Silhouette Intimate Moments® novels** from the Silhouette Reader Service™ **absolutely free!**

There's no catch. You're under no obligation to buy anything. We charge nothing – ZERO – for your first shipment. And you don't have to make any minimum number of purchases – not even one!

Find out for yourself why thousands of readers enjoy receiving books by mail from the Silhouette Reader Service™. They like the **convenience of home delivery**...they like getting the best new novels months before they're available in bookstores...and they love our **discount prices!**

Try us and see! Return this card promptly. We'll send your free books and a free Teddy Bear, under the terms explained on the back. We hope you'll want to remain with the reader service – but the choice is always yours!

345 SDL CTKS
245 SDL CTKM
(S-IM-10/99)

Name: _____
(PLEASE PRINT)

Address: _____ Apt.#: _____

City: _____ State/Prov.: _____ Postal Zip/Code: _____

Offer limited to one per household and not valid to current Silhouette Intimate Moments® subscribers. All orders subject to approval. © 1998 HARLEQUIN ENTERPRISES LTD.
® and ™ are trademarks owned by Harlequin Books S.A. used under license. **PRINTED IN U.S.A.**

▼ CLAIM YOUR FREE BOOKS AND FREE GIFT! RETURN THIS CARD TODAY! ▼

NO OBLIGATION TO BUY!

The Silhouette Reader Service™ — Here's how it works:

There were so many things wrong with that idea, Cade didn't know where to begin. "He's going to want to examine you, take tests—"

Eager, feeling as if she was finally on a positive track, Mac interrupted him. "I'll tell him I've been through entire batteries of tests, and I'm tired of being poked and prodded. I'll flatter him, lay it on thick, saying that someone told me he could put me in touch with a lawyer who—"

"He'd get suspicious," Gray predicted knowingly. "These people can smell a cop a mile away."

That was just the point. "But I'm not a cop," she stressed. "Just a private citizen." The plan began to build momentum in her brain. "Maybe I can bring test results to him—falsified records." She looked at Gray. If doctors were a fraternal organization, the police were even more so. Rules were bent at times for good causes. "You must know somebody who could do that."

It was a good idea, Cade thought. But it needed work. Polishing. "It'd be better if the records were genuine," Cade speculated. Chewing on that corner of the problem, he said slowly, "If we could get our hands on records where the woman was actually infertile—"

Cade stopped, thinking of the doctor back home who had delivered his son. She was a lively woman whose connection with her patients did not end at the edge of the office's boundaries. It was worth a shot.

He looked at Gray. "Can I use your phone?"

Stepping away from the desk, Gray waved at the multilined telephone. Two of the lines weren't lit. "Be my guest."

As Mac listened, Cade called directory assistance in Bedford, California, and asked for the number of Dr. Sheila Pollack. Citing an emergency, he managed to by-pass Sheila's nurse and was talking to her within minutes of dialing.

Piecing things together from his side of the conversation, Mac began to see her idea take shape. She looked at him hopefully when he hung up the telephone.

Cade nodded. "The doctor knows someone. The woman was raped as a teenager and developed endometriosis. Internal scarring prevented her from ever being able to have children. She was around your age when most of the tests were taken." He paused, realizing that McKayla had never actually come out and told him her age. "I'm guessing you're twenty-five."

"Then you're guessing wrong." Although, there was a small part of her that was flattered by the miscalculation. "I'm a dentist, remember? How many twenty-five-year-old dentists do you know?"

"I don't know any dentists," he admitted.

The answer took her by surprise, but it was something she'd get back to later. Right now there was something far more pressing to focus on than Cade's missed visits to the dentist.

"When can we get our hands on the tests?"

"Sheila has to ask the woman for permission, but she doesn't think that should be a problem. If the answer's yes, she'll have her nurse forward them to Megan. Megan'll make the necessary changes so that the records'll look like they're yours." Cade appeared to do a quick calculation. "If all goes well, we can have the records in our hands probably by tomorrow morning.''

The answer disappointed her. She was ready to go ahead with the plan now. ''Tomorrow?''

''It'll probably take you longer than that to get an appointment with the doctor,'' Gray pointed out. He paused, studying her. The woman struck him as being capable enough, but this wasn't simply a challenging situation. She was facing a potentially dangerous one. ''You know what you're getting into?''

Mac didn't hesitate for a moment. ''Yes, the next step to getting Heather back.''

He had a feeling she would say that. Judging by the look on Cade's face, so did he. Gray went over the key points in his mind. ''All right, if you're going to go through with this, may I make a suggestion?''

Cade was open to any input the other man was willing to give them. ''Sure, what?''

''This'll go down a lot better if the two of you show up at the doctor's office together. Mr. and Mrs. Respectable, looking for a baby to round out their perfect lives.''

''Sure,'' Mac agreed. ''That makes sense.'' She looked at Cade. ''Are you willing?''

There was no reason to ask. Cade was going to do whatever it took to recover the little girl. If breaking up a baby-selling ring was included in the deal, so much the better. ''You don't even have to ask.''

It looked as if they had a plan going. Getting into the spirit of it, Gray went on to explore the necessary details.

''I don't doubt that if the good doctor and his wife are involved in a black-market ring, they've been very discreet, very good at what they do. They're not about to take careless chances and get involved in a sting. That means they're going to check you out. You'll need an identity—a life. Here, in Phoenix," he emphasized. "If you say you're from California, it might put them on their guard."

Cade nodded. That made sense. The details could be arranged. "We could tell them I'm an engineer, newly transferred here from the east. We'll need a place to stay—"

Gray was already ahead of him. "One of my wife's friends is a real estate agent. I'll give her a call and see if something can't be arranged for a few days. The main focus is going to be on you in this little drama," Gray warned Mac. He didn't like the idea of a civilian laying herself open like this. "Do you think you're up to it?" Before she could answer, he said, "I can try digging around a little, and if we get more evidence, I might be able to persuade the captain to send in some of our people instead—"

But Mac was shaking her head. "No, all that'll take too much time." She looked to Cade to back her up. "And time's the one thing we don't have. I appreciate anything you can do for us."

"Not a problem." Gray knew he could put in a little time on this case, off duty. Just as backup in case anything happened. That way, the department wouldn't actually be involved.

Mac pulled the telephone over toward her. "I guess I'd better start the ball rolling." Taking a deep breath, she placed the call to the doctor.

Wheels had moved quickly, greased, Mac had a suspicion, by a massive calling in of favors. She'd lost count how many phone calls Cade and Gray had made in the few hours that had followed their initial meeting.

She had a lot of people to be grateful to.

As twilight gave way to night outside, Mac slowly looked around the neat, two-story condominium the real estate agent had found. Furnished, it had just come up on the rental market a week ago. A job transfer had necessitated the owner leaving the country on short notice. He had left everything up to the agency.

The condo was nestled in a pricey neighborhood, making it perfect for their purposes.

In short order, a telephone repairman—someone's brother-in-law—had come after hours to hook them up, allowing another piece of the mosaic to fall into place. The stage was almost set. Even though Dr. Lambert was supposedly booked solid for several months, when she'd heard Mac's address, the receptionist had ''suddenly'' discovered a cancellation and fit them in. They were seeing the doctor tomorrow.

''They shouldn't have much trouble finding someone to lease this,'' she commented.

''Don't be so sure.'' Mac turned from the patio to look at Cade, one brow raised in a silent question. ''It might be a little too close to the railroad tracks to satisfy some people.'' As if to prove his point, a passenger train went by. Even though it was short in comparison to a freight train, the noise and slight swaying that marked its passage underscored Cade's statement.

She grinned. ''You might have something there.''

The smile on his face gave way to concern. He'd

grown accustomed to putting himself on the line, to facing dangerous situations. It was what he was paid for. But she wasn't used to this sort of thing. She was a pediatric dentist, for God's sake. The most dangerous thing she faced was having a patient accidentally bite her. McKayla was diving into this headfirst, and he wondered if she really knew the possible consequences.

"You know, it's not too late to change your mind about this." He saw the surprise in her eyes, but he pressed on. "Once you walk through that door, there'll be no turning back. Lambert hasn't seen you yet. We could still ask the lieutenant to send in someone else."

"No, we couldn't," she insisted. "I don't like sitting on the sidelines, Cade. I *can't* sit on the sidelines. Like you pointed out," she reminded him, "I don't do 'patient' very well."

He was more than aware of that. What he wasn't, he thought, was aware of much else about her beyond the sketchy details he had.

"That you don't," he agreed. "Okay, if you're determined to do this, I'm with you all the way. What we need to do right now is get some dinner and go over your life story."

She looked at him, confused. "You lost me right after the dinner part."

"If we're going to pull this off, you and I are going to have to know more than just each other's names to make it appear as if we're a couple."

Chapter 9

"If you wanted to know something about me, why didn't you just come out and ask?" Mac's smile turned into a grin that included her eyes.

Cade found himself lost in those same eyes for a moment, intrigued and enticed by the glint of humor he saw there. And by the woman who was more than she seemed. While they ate the pizza he'd ordered, Cade had begun with simple questions, working up to complex ones, like why she wasn't married. Clearing his head, he gave a half shrug. "Sorry, let one of my own questions slip through. I'll try to be more careful next time."

His honesty took her aback for a split second. She wasn't expecting it. She felt oddly pleased that he was curious about her.

His asking why she wasn't married made it too personal, he thought. But still, since he'd already begun, he asked, "All right, why didn't you ever get married?"

"I don't think the doctor is going to ask that one. As far as he knows, I *am* married. And for your information, it's personal." And then her eyes laughed at him, giving her away. He looked so serious, as if he didn't know what to do with himself. She'd only meant to tease him. "No, the real reason I never got married was because there just never seemed to be enough time to cultivate a romance."

He thought of his wife. He'd known the first moment he'd seen Elaine that there was something different, something magical there.

A little like there was with McKayla. The realization startled him.

"Sometimes," he said quietly, "it doesn't have to be cultivated, sometimes it just happens."

Something in his tone rippled along Mac's skin, whispering its way into her pores. It unnerved her. Purposely avoiding his eyes, she turned her attention to the half-eaten slice on her plate.

"Well, if it happened, it must have happened while I was busy."

She was far more complex than she let on, Cade thought, but there were pieces that were beginning to emerge for him. Certain givens he had a feeling she guided her life with. "Busy taking care of everyone else?"

Mac looked up sharply. That made her sound domineering and she wasn't. "I don't take care of them—" The quick denial faded a little. "Well, maybe. But that's just the way things arranged themselves."

"Not without help." He smiled knowingly as he picked up his third piece.

Mac dropped the piece back on her plate. Her nerves on edge, she'd been spoiling for a fight, a way to discharge the tension that was knocking around inside her, battering her soul. Cade's comment elected him as her target.

Her eyes narrowed. "What is it that you're suggesting—that I just walk away, not care? Go home and wait for you to call—" Too late, she realized that the words could be taken two ways. The men she knew would have immediately gravitated to the wrong meaning. "To fill me in about the kidnapping," Mac added in a burst of words.

"No, that's not what I meant. I was referring to the rest of it." Cade had gotten the distinct impression that although there appeared to be an outward hierarchy, headed by her father, that the real core of strength for the family was actually Mac. And that perhaps the strain of it was getting to her a little. "I just thought that maybe if you took time out to live your own life, they would be equal to facing theirs."

Annoyed, Mac tried to bridle her irritation. Given the nature of his work, Cade probably thought of himself as part psychologist, but he was way off base here. He hadn't the slightest clue about her or her family. Or the way things were.

"Nice in theory." Mac's words were clipped. "But I wouldn't want to put it into practice."

Cade studied her for a moment. He had a feeling he understood her a little better than she enjoyed being understood. "Afraid to find out that they can stand up on their own two feet without you?"

No. The single word rushed to Mac's lips, but in all fairness, she suppressed it and thought over what he'd said. And discovered that there was a small part of her that was afraid, afraid of not being needed. Being needed had become a very large part of her life, a part she wasn't sure she could completely exist without.

"Maybe," she agreed. And then her eyes held his. "But more afraid of seeing them fall on their faces—or worse—because I wasn't there as a backup."

Cade wondered if she actually believed that, or if it was just something she was telling herself. And yet, she didn't strike him as someone who had to be constantly in control because it fed an inner need for empowerment. It was more of a situation that she'd allowed to happen, for one reason or another.

"To be a backup, you have to stand back," he reminded her with a smile. "Not lead the way."

Maybe he was right, and maybe he wasn't, but Mac wasn't feeling her sharpest right now and she wasn't up to matching wits with him. So she sidelined the debate by restating her position. "Say what you want, Cade, I'm not going home now. Not when we're this close."

Picking up a napkin, Cade wiped off his fingers. For now, three slices were enough. He noticed that she was still trifling with her first one. That wasn't good. "No one's telling you to. I don't think the doctor would believe that I was the one who wanted to get pregnant."

The image of his sitting in the doctor's office, confiding this secret desire to be pregnant, had Mac laughing out loud.

Suddenly, a piece of the pizza slice became lodged in her windpipe. Within seconds, the laughter turned to panic. No air was coming in, and she couldn't cough up the piece. Her eyes widened as the horror of the situation penetrated. She was going to choke to death.

Cade saw the look in her eyes and immediately reacted. Getting up from the table so fast that his chair fell backward, he came up behind her and yanked Mac to her feet. He encircled her rib cage with his arms. With his hands clasped just beneath her breastbone, Cade applied pressure quickly, jerking upward hard. Her back was pressed against his chest, and even in the midst of the dire situation, he was aware of her hair brushing along his face, aware of the scent of it.

Jerking again, afraid he was going to wind up injuring her ribs, he squeezed even harder. The next moment, the piece came flying out.

Making noises like a woman who'd just been pulled from a watery grave, Mac gulped in snatches of air. Concerned, relieved, Cade held her for a moment to see if she could stand on her own.

He held her, he thought later, perhaps a second too long. Just long enough for him to realize that his hands were pressed against her breasts and that the very contact that had given her air had sucked it away from him.

A light-headedness filtered through him. Cade attributed it to McKayla's narrow escape. "Are you all right?"

The question seemed to rumble along her back at the same time that the breath that propelled it brushed along the top of her head, tingling her scalp. Mac could feel everything tightening inside of her, like skin reacting to a sudden, unexpected sweet breeze.

"Uh-huh." Pulling herself together, she took another deep breath, embarrassed, but for the most part relieved. Turning so that she faced him, her lips curved in a half smile.

"I guess I can always do that if the doctor starts asking too many questions."

"Hell of a conversation stopper," he observed.

He was still holding her, Cade realized. Only now, his hands were at her back. Wound a little too close, a little too tight. Telling himself it was to give her support didn't exactly have the ring of truth to it. Even he saw through it.

"Um, Cade?" Mac began. She licked her lower lip, catching it between her teeth as she looked up at him.

He found himself fighting against urges that suddenly popped out of nowhere, demanding attention. Demanding satisfaction. He barely trusted his voice as he replied, "Yes?"

The tiniest of smiles seeped into her eyes again, finding its way to her mouth. "How long are you going to go on holding me?"

He considered lying, mumbling some excuse, or just dropping his hands. None of the above seemed to work. He fell back on the truth. It was his only option. "Until I either let you go, or kiss you."

Her lips curved a little more, entirely without her permission. Mac's heart refused to calm down, continuing the strange rhythm it had started when he'd taken her in his arms. "I see. Have you made up your mind which it's going to be?"

"Just about there." Cade whispered the words a heartbeat before he lowered his mouth to hers.

This was asking for trouble, she knew that. It just further complicated an already-complicated situation unnecessarily. Kissing him was clearly the wrong thing at the wrong time, and yet she couldn't follow through on her thoughts, couldn't quite make herself move away.

Couldn't quite make herself not enjoy what was happening, or the effect it was having on her even while she was attempting to argue herself out of it.

Like the lens of a camera zeroing in on a close-up, the instant his lips touched hers, everything else around her went out of focus. All she could think of was Cade, the hard press of his body against hers. The way he held her, as if she were something fragile, something that could break.

Ever since she could remember, Mac had always prided herself on her strength of character, her ability to stand up to anything that came her way, large or small. She truly liked the fact that her family turned to her in their time of need. Every time. But it would have been a lie to deny that there was something incredibly enticing about being held this way, kissed this way. As if she needed to be cared for.

Maybe she'd been deprived of oxygen longer than she'd thought.

This was a first, Cade realized. He'd never mixed business with pleasure before, never taken pleasure in his business outside of having a job well done to his credit. But there was pleasure here, deep, dark, over-whelming pleasure that drew him down to a place he hadn't been in a very long time, while sending a rush through his veins.

He couldn't even say what it was about McKayla that unstrung him this way, making him do things he deemed not only out of line, but also completely unprofessional. But there was definitely something.

Something.

Deepening the kiss, he cupped the back of her head, wishing he never had to let go.

The woman went through life like gangbusters, a bright flare that shot off and lit the sky. And yet, there was something in the heart of the light show she created that gave him pause, that made him believe the lady was not completely tough, completely invincible, the way she wanted everyone to believe she was.

If he didn't know better, he would have said she was even vulnerable.

There'd be no pulling back in a moment if she didn't stop now, Mac thought. In another second, she was going to be sucked in by the vortex, and then who knew what was going to happen? She was just barely holding on to her sensibilities now.

She took a breath, trying to steady a pulse that could no longer be counted on to be measured by any medical instrument known to man.

The breath didn't help.

"Boy, when you make up your mind to do something, you go right out and do it with a vengeance, don't you?" Mac asked when she finally managed to end the kiss. Her eyes searched his face for answers to questions she couldn't even completely form in her mind. She couldn't remember ever feeling this un-

steady before, like someone trying to get their footing
while standing on a mound of gelatin. "Was that your
idea of mouth-to-mouth resuscitation?"

Humor glinted in his eyes. Cade had come very
close to breaking every rule he'd made for himself.
Rules that he'd never had to even mildly contemplate
enforcing before. "Maybe."

"Which of us were you resuscitating?"

Cade slowly swept tentative fingers along her
cheek, brushing back hair he'd mussed. Savoring the
feel of her. Wishing he could indulge more, knowing
he shouldn't. "I'm not sure." He was right, she
looked as shaken, as unsure as he felt. "Both, I
think."

Her eyes held his for a long time. Touched by the
humor, she felt like a flower being coaxed open beneath a warm sun. Still, she knew there was a step to
be taken here, but whether it should be forward or
backward, she wasn't certain. Nor did she know anymore if it was her choice or his. What had he done
to her?

"So now what?"

It was up to him, Cade thought. Up to him to set
the tone and create the distance. Because he'd been
the one to shatter it. Forcing himself to release her,
he backed away. Then, bending down, he picked up
her chair before reaching for his own. "We get back
to finding things out about each other." He sat down
again.

"I think we just did," she murmured under her
breath.

He heard her. "You're right, maybe that is enough
for now. We can get back to this—to talking," he

interjected when he realized that she might think he meant to take what had just happened between them to its logical conclusion.

Nothing logical about blowing up the known world and starting again from scratch, he told himself.

She was nodding, finishing his statement for him before he had the chance. "After the appointment tomorrow."

"Exactly."

Except it wasn't exactly what he wanted to say, Cade thought, because it wasn't what he meant. And if he wasn't completely mistaken, neither did she.

The digital display on the bedside clock showed that it was two o'clock. Three minutes past two, to be exact. Mac hadn't had a wink of sleep since she'd retired to her room.

More like "retreated," Mac thought, disgusted with herself. What was the matter with her, anyway? This wasn't about her, or the funny way she was feeling, it was about Heather and recovering her. And *only* about Heather. She should be out there, laying strategy, not in here, doing an imitation of a spinning top.

She was too wound up to sleep. Again. And this time, if she were being honest with herself, it wasn't just because of Heather's kidnapping. If this kept up, she was going to turn into a zombie, looking exactly like one of the walking dead. She wished there was a pool around. Maybe if she did a hundred laps, she'd be able to fall asleep and get at least a few minutes in before they had to get going again.

She glanced toward the common wall she and Cade

were sharing. A thousand laps was more like it, she amended ruefully. Without meaning to, she touched her fingers to her lips. And quietly sighed.

A few minutes later, she heard Cade knock on her door. As she opened it, she dragged her other hand through the hair hanging in her eyes, and blinked un-comprehendingly as she looked at him.

She looked more tired than Cade had expected. He'd listened to her restless movements for as long as he could before he'd gotten up to check on her. It made him want to take her into his arms again. *Careful, Townsend, that's what started all this in the first place.* "Anything I can help with?"

"Excuse me?"

He nodded toward the bed behind her. It looked like the scene of an unresolved skirmish. "You've been prowling around in here like a caged tiger for the last few hours. Is there anything I can do?"

No, you've already done enough, Mac thought.

She shook her head. "You're doing as much as you can." She had to blame this on something and said the first believable thing that came to mind. "Just opening-night jitters, I guess."

The fact that she was admitting to a weakness, an insecurity, told him that he had suddenly found himself in a very rare club. He had a feeling Mac was showing him a side of herself that others rarely got to see.

By nature, he wasn't a demonstrative man. He didn't fall into the touchy-feely category that so many others of his acquaintance were in. So it caught him as much by surprise as it did Mac when he covered her hand with his. "You'll be fine."

Mac's mind reverted back to the real problem. She wished she could believe that, she thought. Wished that she could believe that all this would have a happy ending. That she could give Heather back to her sister.

It was the uncertainty of it that was driving her crazy.

Breaking contact, she moved toward the one large window in the bedroom. She stared out but only saw miles and miles of desert.

Trying not to shiver, Mac ran her hands up along her arms. "I don't know." That sounded so shaky, she thought, but she just couldn't help herself. She was afraid. Really afraid. Needing something to hang on to, she turned toward him. "What if I—"

Cade knew where this was going. Had taken the journey himself. He placed his finger to her lips, silencing the doubt, not letting it emerge.

"The what-ifs will drive you crazy if you let them." His eyes were kind as he smiled into hers. "The trick is not to let them. Worrying is just wasting energy that could be put to better use."

For the second time that day, Mac felt her heart stop. Or did this count as two days? She didn't know, and she didn't really care. What mattered was the man standing before her, offering her hope. Asking for nothing in return. Making her want to give so much.

"Just what sort of use did you have in mind?" Was that her asking that question, or was she just thinking it? She couldn't tell.

Oh, there were things he wanted to do with her, Cade thought. Wild, impossible, head-spinning, mind-blowing things that he couldn't allow himself to even think about, much less indulge in. So instead, he ran his fingers along her cheek, cupping it for a moment, letting the softness of her skin seep into his consciousness before withdrawing his hand.

"Anyone ever tell you that you ask too many questions?"

Mac suddenly realized exactly what she wanted from him, and it startled her. She wanted a haven from the storm swirling around her. A reprieve from her thoughts. All of them. Did that make her weak? Was she failing someone by feeling this way? "How else am I going to learn?"

Oh, God, Cade had never been this tempted before, never felt desire knocking so hard against his paper-thin door. For two cents...

No, not for all the money in the world. He'd be guilty of violating a trust. Hers—and his in his own integrity.

"Some things are better left alone, McKayla. Now, get some sleep." He was already backing away. Backing away before he forgot all his own promises and took her the way everything within him begged him to.

The room was meant to put the occupants who crossed its threshold at ease. So was the manner of the distinguished, hospitable older man who was sitting behind his sturdy oak desk, talking to them.

If she didn't know any better, Mac would have sworn she'd made a mistake.

But she did know better. And she had to hang on to that thought. That, and the fact that she, that *they* were going to get Heather back.

"A great many women who have sat in that chair have said the very same things to me, Mrs. Sinclair." With an encouraging smile, Dr. Erasmus Lambert looked directly into Mac's eyes.

If there was a smoother liar in the world, she didn't want to meet him, Mac thought.

She'd just spent the last twenty-five minutes "pouring out her heart" to a man who could have easily played Father Christmas in the next holiday pageant. Kindly, with a full head of white hair, Dr. Lambert had possibly the friendliest face she had ever seen. She could see how others could be so easily taken in by him. He projected a compassion that soundlessly and quickly destroyed all barriers between the patient and himself, simultaneously turning him into a father confessor and granter of dreams all in the same breath.

Putting the proper hitch in her voice, Mac reached for Cade's hand as she continued looking at Lambert. "And did they all become mothers?"

Lambert's smile was almost beatific as it shone on her. "Eventually."

Playing the part of the skeptical husband, Cade challenged him with just the proper touch of hope in his voice. "You have that much of a success rate?"

Lambert leaned back and gestured at the bulletin board behind him. Photographs of newborns and toddlers overlapped one another in a gay profusion of silent laughter as well as happiness.

"In one way or another."

Raising her chin defensively, Mac said, "Then I'll have to be 'another.'" Slanting only a cursory glance toward Cade, she went into the story they had rehearsed. "I can't have children, Doctor. I was raped when I was twenty." Her voice quavering, Mac paused before continuing. It wasn't her story. It belonged to a woman named Julia Sinclair. A woman as it turned out to be, in an odd quirk of fate that told her they were all somehow interrelated in this world, Kane Madigan's sister-in-law. "The man was someone I knew. I was too ashamed to go to the police, to even tell anyone until it was too late."

"Too late?" There was nothing but compassion in his voice.

Biting her lower lip, Mac nodded as Cade clasped her hand in his. She purposely avoided the doctor's eyes in a show of embarrassment. "The infection I came down with evolved into endometriosis." Peripherally, she saw the older man nodding his head. "I've been to a dozen specialists and they've all said that I...that I can't have children." Twisting on the wedding ring she had recently put on to complete the part, she paused, swallowing a sob. Under control, Mac raised her eyes to Lambert's. "I've come to you looking for a miracle."

"In vitro pregnancies are science, not miracles, Mrs. Sinclair, but—"

"We've tried that as well," Cade said. He shook his head. "It didn't work. All it did was raise my wife's hopes over and over again, just to shatter them. I don't want her going through any more grief."

"I see."

Pressing her lips together, Mac forged ahead. "I know I can never carry a baby within my body, Doctor. I've accepted that. But I do want to carry one in my arms. My husband and I desperately want to adopt a baby.''

''And you've come to me because—''

''Because we've heard that we stand a better chance attempting a private adoption,'' Cade told him. ''The regular route would take years, and I might not have years, Doctor.''

''I beg your pardon?'' Lambert frowned.

It was Mac's turn to cut in. Together they were attempting to behave like a couple who knew each other well enough to finish each other's sentences. ''My husband has been diagnosed with a heart condition, Doctor. No official agency is going to allow a child to be placed with a family where the father has already had one heart attack and might have another, more fatal one.'' Clutching Cade's hand, she leaned forward on the edge of her seat. ''You are our only hope, Dr. Lambert.''

Very slowly, Lambert nodded. ''Adoption agencies want only the best for the children they place—''

''We can give the child the best. The best love, the best home, the best of everything. We have the money. Just because something 'might' happen years down the line—and might not—is not a reason to deny us the love of a child, or a child our love.'' Mac's voice vibrated with passion.

''Very well put, Mrs. Sinclair.'' Rising from his seat, the doctor crossed to her and placed a comforting hand on her shoulder. ''I'm on your side,'' he assured her. ''As a matter of fact, my wife and I found ourselves in the exact same position you are in some years ago. That was how I got into this area to begin with. Because I understand what it feels like to be deprived of something that is so very basic to the perpetuation of the family—a child.'' He paused, looking from Cade to Mac. ''You're completely certain you don't want to try in vitro—''

''Positive,'' Mac cut in. ''I don't think I could stand facing the disappointment again. It's like having my heart slashed out of my chest.'' Thinking of Heather, her eyes filled with tears. ''I've been through it so many times before.''

Lambert looked at her with sympathy. ''I understand.''

''I was hoping you'd say that. You're the answer to a prayer, Doctor.''

The smile on Lambert's lips told Mac that he thought of himself in exactly the same light.

Chapter 10

"So now we play the waiting game?" Mac asked under her breath as Cade walked out with her from the eighth-floor office.

They had just spent the last hour with the doctor, answering questions, filling out forms and filling in gaps of information. The parade of questions began to seem endless, but they'd met the challenge. At the end of the session, Lambert had told him he felt confident that there was a child in their near future. He escorted them to his inner office door, saying he would be in touch. When Mac had pressed for a date, he had only said "soon."

Walking beside her, Cade could see that Mac was having trouble containing her agitation. Not that he could blame her. He'd feel the same way in her position. He would have sold his soul to be in her position.

He pressed for the elevator. "That's the plan."

"I'm not sure I can wait."

With his hand on the small of her back, he ushered her in as the doors drew back. There was no one else in the car. "We have no alternative."

Mac stared at Lambert's office door as the elevator doors closed. She wanted to push the doors apart and run back into the office.

"Why can't we just go in and get him? Get them all?" That made sense, didn't it? They had the proof they needed. And she had noticed that there were two young nurses in the office, neither of whom matched the DMV photograph they had. It only reinforced the feeling for Mac that they were running out of time. "He's got Heather. If we lose him—"

Even though they were the only ones on the elevator, Cade kept his voice low. "Redhawk has men watching both offices and Lambert's home." To keep up the charade, and because he felt she needed some show of comfort, Cade placed his arm around her shoulders. "There're no babies going anywhere without either his or one of his men knowing it, McKayla."

The doors opened. Mac walked out, feeling as if she was in a daze, operating on automatic pilot. "But Redhawk said he couldn't—"

"Unofficially," Cade said significantly. Looking around, he located his car and began to walk toward it. "He has people working on the case when they're officially off duty, as a favor to him. And Redhawk's doing it as a favor to Kane."

It was just as Mac had thought earlier. She had a great many people to be grateful to.

They walked slowly toward the rented car. All around them, there were cars cruising the heavily trafficked lot, looking for parking spaces. Cade wondered if one of the cars seemingly meandering belonged to someone who was actually in the process of tailing them. It wouldn't have taken long to get the word out, and Lambert had stepped out of the room for several minutes while they were filling out forms.

Mac stopped at their car. "And there's no getting in contact with Lieutenant Redhawk for us?"

Reaching over, Cade unlocked the passenger door for her. "Not physically. We can still call him—from a pay phone."

Mac sat down, turning to look at Cade as he slid in behind the wheel. "He couldn't have the cell phones bugged—"

He never made the mistake of underestimating the enemy. Until Darin was taken from him, he'd gone through life with blinders on. But the blinders were now permanently off.

Cade laughed softly to himself. "It's easier picking up the signal from a cell phone than you'd imagine."

Mac shook her head, buckling up as he started the car. "All this intrigue makes my life as a dentist seem pretty tame."

He laughed. "Oh, I don't know, I can remember when going to the dentist seemed pretty dramatic to me."

"Exactly how long ago was that?"

"Long enough," he admitted. "Tell you what, when this is all over, why don't you throw in an initial dental exam as part of my fee?"

It was Mac's turn to laugh as she tried to picture

him in her office. There were cartoon posters on the walls and a fresh, endless supply of kiddie videos to distract her young patients. "I'll do better than that. You help me find Heather and your teeth are going to be taken care of for life."

Cade was about to tell her that he was kidding, but then let it go. Maybe it wouldn't be such a bad idea at that, seeing her after this was over—with a good excuse handy if he wanted to use it.

"Got yourself a deal."

Twisting in her seat, Mac looked out the back window. "Do you think we're being followed?"

He was more than sure. He would have bet his life on it. "Look behind you."

"That blue car?"

That would have been too obvious. They weren't dealing with an amateur. But then, he wasn't one anymore, either. "No, the beige one behind it. It's been with us since we left." He'd noticed it as one of the cars circling the lot when they went to their car. "I'm sure that Lambert and his lawyer friend take no chances."

"What about the kidnapping? I'd think that kidnapping a child under the noses of everyone would be taking a damn big chance."

His guess was that Heather's kidnapping had been a plan that had gone awry at the last minute. "Calculated risk," he pointed out. "There's a difference."

Cade glanced at the rearview mirror. The car was keeping up a steady pace. He changed lanes. A beat later, so did the man in the beige car.

Point proved, he thought.

"I'm going to have Sam's wife look into it for us,

but I'm sure that most of the adoptions coming out of the lawyer's office are legal.'' If not most, then half, he amended. ''Maybe they were all legitimate once, but the demand for adoptable children is a high one. It probably proved to be too much of a temptation for Lambert and Taylor after a while. It's hard to turn your back on a lucrative business.''

The idea that something involving children's lives, and the lives of their families, could be thought of as a business chilled Mac's heart at the same time that it infuriated her.

With effort, she tried to focus on what he was saying. ''Sam's wife?''

''Savannah Walters can probably hack into any system in the country if she put her mind to it.''

Mac wasn't sure if that was a recommendation or not. But at this point, she realized that they needed all the help they could get.

''Professional thief?'' she guessed.

Thief would have been the last word Cade would have ever thought of using to describe Savannah. If he had to use one, it would have been *lady*. It was written all over her.

''No, just a computer genius. Even better than Megan, which amazes me.'' He took his hat off to anyone who knew their way around that mysterious world. ''My expertise with the computer is confined to using a single form of word processing and occasionally surfing the Web for ten minutes at a time.'' He grinned, glancing in her direction. ''Some people might call me a dinosaur.''

''Not if they've ever kissed you,'' Mac muttered under her breath as she turned her head away.

But he heard her. And he smiled.

Hanging up, Cade looked thoughtfully at the telephone he'd just used. He wasn't staring at the phone, but at the chrome plate on the bottom. He could see the driver of the beige car following them, on foot, around the mall.

"It's what I thought," Cade whispered, slipping an arm around Mac. "Taylor has a P.I. he keeps on constant retainer. I'd say that we've become his new assignment." He'd called Savannah with his suspicions, and given her the car's license number, then hung on while she'd checked it out. She'd given him a quick description of the man, having pulled up a photograph from the licensing bureau. Pretending to nuzzle Mac, he continued talking. "Going by what Savannah told me, I'd say our man is that tall guy over there, the one sipping a cup of overpriced coffee."

Mac stole a glance, trying not to be obvious. The man in question was sitting at a small table for one just outside Café Delight. He appeared engrossed in his newspaper, but she didn't doubt Cade's instincts for a second.

She couldn't help smiling at his wording, though. "I take it you don't care very much for those new kinds of coffee."

Cade shrugged. "To me, there're only two kinds. Good and bad."

Her smile grew. "And a good cup of coffee would be—?"

"Hot. Black. Strong. Otherwise, what's the point?" He'd been drinking his coffee that way ever since he was fourteen, he saw no reason to change now. If it wasn't broken, there was no purpose in fixing something.

"Enjoyment," Mac suggested. Being open to new things was what made life exciting.

"I enjoy hot and strong."

Why was he looking at her when he said that? Cade suddenly wondered. And then he knew. It was because the two adjectives could be applied to her as easily as they could to the coffee.

Blocking his thoughts, he nodded toward the mall exit. "Let's go."

Mac was beginning to like the feel of his arm around her shoulders and to like the realization that they were walking in as close to a syncopated gait as she'd ever managed. Trying not to think about it only made her think about it that much more.

Keep your mind on your reason for being here, she told herself.

When she turned her head toward Cade to ask him a question, she found that their faces were much too close for comfort. And that their lips were closer than was healthy for her.

She thought of the man behind them. Were they succeeding in fooling him? Their act was certainly beginning to fool her. "So now that we've acquired this tail to our kite, what do we do?"

"Act naturally. Go through the paces of a loving couple yearning for a child." They were passing a clothing store for toddlers. This was the kind of signpost the P.I. would be looking for. Cade purposely stopped. "Go window-shopping in hopes of having someone to wear things like that very soon."

He looked at her and saw that there were tears sliding down her cheek. Stunned at the depth of her ability to take over a part, Cade fished a handkerchief out of his pocket and handed it to her.

Pretending to comfort her, he whispered, "You don't need to get that far into the role."

"I'm not," she sniffed after she'd collected herself. "I just bought that outfit for Heather as a Christmas gift. The day before...before..." Mac exhaled loudly, looking away. "I'm sorry, I don't usually cry."

The sight of her tears made him feel helpless. He hated feeling helpless. "For what it's worth, you've probably impressed the P.I. with your sincerity. He'll undoubtedly go back to his boss saying we're the genuine article and that you want a baby so much you burst into tears at the very sight of a mannequin dressed in a little girl's overalls." He wanted to get out of here, to go someplace where she could relax and feel free to be herself. "C'mon, let me take you back to the condo."

Lacing his fingers with hers, Cade walked out of the mall and toward the parking structure with her.

"I didn't mean to break down like that before," she finally said, looking at him.

"You don't have to apologize." Hearing the apology only made him feel uncomfortable for her. "I never had you pegged as a robot, anyway."

"What did you have me pegged as?"

"A very strong woman." Watching the traffic ahead, he spared her a glance and saw that his answer had pleased her. He'd expected as much. "But even strong women can take a break now and then. Be human. Otherwise they wind up breaking."

"And you'd be an expert on the subject?" she asked, appearing grateful for the break in tension.

He knew it was a teasing question, but he answered it seriously. "In a way. My wife Elaine was a strong woman." Cade didn't realize that his jaw hardened just a little as he added, "Especially toward the end."

"The end?" His profile was almost rigid. Was he talking about a divorce, or something more permanent? Mac bit her lip, knowing she shouldn't have asked.

"She died of cancer." Even now the words still shook Cade down to the core, despite his attempts to separate himself from the reality. "Found out in June, was gone six weeks to the day. The disease attacked her body with a vengeance—but not her spirit."

Mac could hear his pain, though he tried to disguise it. It made her feel like an intruder, but a tiny part of her was glad that he had shared this with her. "I'm sorry, I didn't mean to pry."

He shrugged away her apology. Cade scanned the road. He vaguely remembered there being a supermarket somewhere in the vicinity.

"That's all right. Maybe I should have talked about her a little more." *Instead of blocking out the ordeal and Elaine's death,* he added silently. Spotting the building, he guided the car over to the right lane. "She was a hell of a woman." He glanced at Mac. "So are you."

That was entirely unexpected. About to shrug away the compliment, Mac stopped and allowed herself to enjoy it instead. The smile was quick, flashing across her lips like lightning across a summer sky that couldn't quite come to terms with a sudden shift in the weather.

"Thanks."

He nodded. "Don't mention it." He brought the car to a stop.

Mac's eyes narrowed as she looked around the busy parking lot. "What are we doing here?"

He was already out of the car, rounding the hood to her side. "Shopping. We're not newlyweds, so I think they expect us to live on food instead of love." Without looking up, using only his peripheral vision, Cade saw that the beige car had pulled up and parked two rows over.

Good call, he congratulated himself as they headed into the store and grabbed a shopping cart.

He hadn't expected it to bring back memories, but it did. Wandering up and down the aisles of a supermarket beside a woman pushing a grocery cart aroused bittersweet feelings within him as it ushered back fragments of the past. Cade was acutely reminded of late, harried Friday evenings when he and Elaine would meet after work and do the week's grocery shopping before heading home to settle in for two days of catching up with their lives. And two days of lovemaking.

When Darin had come along, Elaine quit her job, but the process remained essentially the same. And each Friday evening, like clockwork, they would go shopping for groceries.

Mac noticed the look on his face. "Is anything wrong?"

It took him several minutes before he could successfully block out his pain. Finally, Cade shook his head. "Just remembering something, that's all."

Subtly, she glanced over her shoulder, but she had a feeling he wasn't referring to their newly acquired shadow. Cade's expression stuck in her mind long after they had hit the checkout line and walked out of the store.

"*Was* something bothering you back there?" Mac asked the question as they were taking bags of groceries out of the trunk and carrying them into the condo. She knew she was prying again, but she couldn't get the expression he'd worn out of her mind.

Unlocking the front door, Cade shouldered it open and walked to the kitchen table with the groceries before he said anything. He debated making something up, but nothing came to him that would fit the occasion. He fell back on what he'd said before. "No, nothing was bothering me. I was just remembering, that's all."

He was putting borders up around himself, Mac thought as she began to unpack the bags. Which shouldn't have bothered her at all, seeing as how they were supposed to be involved in only a professional way.

But the trouble was their involvement had begun to leak into other parts of her life. What was evolving was something that wasn't nearly as antiseptically professional as she would have liked....

Actually, she amended, maybe the involvement *was* more professional than she would have liked. She realized with a start, as she forced herself to continue putting groceries away in the walk-in pantry, that there was something about this man, as much as she tried to actively deny it, that got to her. Something about him that reached out to her. Had been reaching out to her all along.

She had no idea if it was her perpetual do-gooder complex that had her seeing him as a man who needed someone, or if it was that for once in her life, she was willing to admit, at least partially, that she needed someone herself.

Now there was a switch, her needing someone. The thought made her uncomfortable with herself. Walking out of the pantry, she almost bumped into Cade. Startled, she stepped back and looked at him. He had a can of coffee in each hand.

"Two?" They weren't about to stay here long enough to need two cans no matter how strong he took his coffee.

He shrugged. "They were on sale."

The thought amused her. "A man who shops for bargains—you're incredible." She paused, the smile mellowing into something a little more serious. "Do you want to talk about it?"

He stacked one can on top of another. "What, buying two cans of coffee?"

"No, whatever it was that you remembered…earlier, in the store." She kept adding words, her momentum failing, as he looked at her.

"Not particularly."

His tone told her to back off—politely. She dug in instead. It was her way. She left a bag of Fuji apples on the table to fend for themselves. "Maybe you should, anyway."

He looked at her. "What makes you say that?"

"Well, it's obvious that what it reminded you of was something about your wife, and you said talking about her makes her come to life for you. Maybe you need to let her do that, for a little while." The look in his eyes made her falter just a little. They'd turned dark. She pressed on, confident she was right. "It helps you move on if you examine your feelings."

The last thing Cade wanted right now was pop psychology.

"I don't have to examine them. I know exactly what my feelings are. I loved her, and she's gone. And I get to move through life alone—looking for the son we created." He didn't realize he was raising his voice until he'd finished.

Mac blew out a breath. "Well, I guess that puts me in my place, doesn't it?"

He hadn't meant to sound off at her. He'd thought he had better control over himself than that. But he'd been feeling a little on edge the last twenty-four hours or so. He took out a box of instant mashed potatoes and flattened the empty bag.

"Sorry, I didn't mean to snap."

"You didn't." Mac took the bag from his hand and automatically put it in a drawer, the way she did at home. "Snapping is what my father does. You were just firmly stating your point—and posting a ten-foot No Trespassing sign in front of you. I'm the one who should apologize. I should have respected your boundaries."

Cade didn't want her apologizing to him, not when he was the one who nearly took off her head. She could call it what she would, he knew what he was guilty of. And he knew why, too.

He put his hands on her shoulders to keep her in place while he talked. It was easier talking to the back of her head, but he wasn't interested in taking the easy way.

"Look, this is a little hard for me right now. I don't know why, but being with you reminds me of being with Elaine. It's different, but the same—" He searched her face, trying to see if he was getting through. "Does that make any sense?"

"It could—" Her eyes held his for a minute. "If you're saying what I think you're saying."

He'd already gone too far. Cade dropped his hands to his side. "Maybe we should just leave it that way, unsaid."

"Are you afraid, Cade?" she asked, smiling.

There was no shame in a healthy dose of fear. Fear kept you alive to come back and fight the good fight another day. "Yeah, maybe I am."

"Of what?"

The question was a whisper that teased his very soul.

He couldn't be anything but honest. Anything else wouldn't have been him. "Of you. Of feeling this way. Of feeling anything at all."

"Why?"

Why couldn't he just keep his mind on what he was sent here to do? Why couldn't he focus, the way he always could before? She was messing with his mind, and she wasn't even trying.

"Because feelings aren't selective. You open yourself up to them, and a whole bunch of things can come pouring in. Pain as well as pleasure.''

"Some people might say that's a fair price to pay."

There was nothing fair about the price. "Some people haven't lost as much as I have."

Courage was never something Mac had to search for. Until now. She grasped at what she could find and pushed on, all the while afraid to go on, more afraid to stop after she'd come this far.

"Some people would say that you've had a lot to lose, but that at least you had it."

Cade heard something telling in her voice. Something that shortened the gap between them even more. "You've never loved anyone?"

Mac refused to look away, even though she wanted to. "My family."

"But never—"

"I said no, didn't I?" She realized that she was now the one who was being defensive, but she couldn't seem to help herself. "There's never been that special someone in my life. Nobody ever made my pulse race, my breath stop, my head spin—"

Until now.

Because she knew she was describing things that Cade did to her. For her. But that was something she didn't intend to say out loud. It was bad enough that he could probably see it in her eyes.

Turning away, she began to move back toward the table and the remaining bag. "The ice cream's melting."

"We didn't buy any ice cream." But even as Cade said it, he wasn't completely certain. After he'd remembered shopping with Elaine, the rest had been a hazy blur.

"Yes, we did." Taking out the container, she placed it in the freezer. "I snuck it in when you weren't looking."

That wasn't the only thing she had snuck in when he wasn't looking, he realized. Because while he hadn't been looking, hadn't been anticipating, McKayla had somehow managed to sneak in beyond the fences he kept up. Snuck into a region that he liked to keep strictly free, strictly open.

Mac felt him looking at her. Turning toward him, she was suddenly unsure again. Taking a stroll over a tightrope without even making sure it was properly strung up from here to there.

She ran her tongue over her dry bottom lip. "Is there something I can do for you?"

"Yes," he said softly, "there is."

"What?"

Mystified, Cade heard himself saying words that were forming without his conscious consent. "Make me forget everything I just said."

Mac wondered if he could hear her heart beating. "I don't know if I can."

"I think, for once in your life, you've underestimated yourself, McKayla," he said as his arms closed around her.

Chapter 11

If Mac underestimated herself, she underestimated the effect Cade would have on her even more.

From the moment she willingly stepped out of the safeguards she'd created for herself, she was completely lost. From the instant his lips touched hers, she was found again. Found, but in such a very different way.

Everything in her world changed.

Everything that had been so orderly, so mapped out even in the midst of the chaos swirling around her, fell apart as if it had been just so many scrapings brushed off the surface of a burned piece of toast. Specks flying into the wind.

He made her blood sing to a tune she'd always suspected was out there somewhere, but had never heard before.

First slowly, then with more feeling, more depth,

Cade's lips claimed hers, taking her out of the enclosed four walls of the house where they were pretending to be married and into the skies.

Taking her out of herself.

She could feel her body quickening, ripening. Yearning for him even as they just stood there in the kitchen, held fast in place by passions that had been a long time in coming.

She felt so fragile in his hands, so fragile against his body, Cade was afraid he'd break her if he wasn't careful. And wouldn't she just love to know that? She sped through life like a runaway train, yet he couldn't shake the image of someone delicate beneath the smoke and noise.

The length and breadth of his desire was suddenly so huge, so unmanageable and oh, so definitely in the driver's seat. It took every last bit of restraint he had not to just scoop her up in his arms and carry her off to the bedroom to make love with her.

The way he wanted to.

But each kiss took him farther away from the center of his control, farther into the inferno he'd uncovered just beneath the surface. The one that threatened to engulf them both.

Heart pounding, Cade ran his hands along her supple, sleek body. Assuring himself that this was real, that it wasn't just something that had materialized from nowhere in the middle of the night, shrouded in a misty dream to slip into his sleep to taunt him and remind him that once he'd been a man, with a man's appetites, a man's hunger. A man's needs.

Needs.

The word sprang up at him in big, bold letters, only

to be consumed the next moment by the fire flaring from within.

Needs. He needed her.

The realization occurred to him, even as he struggled to understand, to make sense of the implications. He hadn't needed, hadn't allowed himself to need, anyone for a very long time.

Needing brought vulnerability and pain in its wake, sweeping away everything that came before and leaving only ashes in its wake.

And yet...

But that was for later, when he could think. When ramifications joined hands with consequences to haunt and taunt, and weigh heavily on his mind. That wasn't for now.

Now was for loving.

For feeling.

For touching.

He heard Mac's sharp intake of breath as he pulled her to him even more, molding her body to his and his to hers. The fit was perfect.

As was the woman.

Mac gave herself up to him, to the sensations racing around inside, screaming for release. More than for release, for validation. Begging for it.

And for more.

She could feel her body vibrating in delicious, burning anticipation with each pass of Cade's hands, each kiss that singed her skin. Mac was vaguely aware that he was peeling her clothes away, not roughly the way she would have expected a man to do, but gently, as if each layer was made of delicate parchment that would give way and tear if he moved too quickly.

First her blouse left her body, then her skirt, then the straps of her bra, which he moved aside bit by torturous bit. As if to tease them both. Prime them both.

By the time she felt the clasp release at her back, she was vibrating like a tuning fork and her breath was something she had only a nodding acquaintance with. It barely remained within her lungs long enough to keep her conscious before it whooshed away again.

She'd never felt this way before. *And would never feel this way again.* That certainty brought a bittersweet sadness with it that she would have found intolerable if she'd only been able to retain it long enough to remember.

But he swept everything in his path away with the touch of his hand, with the press of his lips.

She curled her arms around his neck, her head dropping back as he wove a ring of light, feathery kisses around the base of her throat. She could feel her pulse jumping, could feel the bra slipping away.

She couldn't be nude when he was still dressed. The thought intruded suddenly, prying apart the almost-solid waves of heat surrounding her brain. Coming to life, Mac began working the buttons of his shirt out of their holes, her fingertips numb.

None gave way, stubbornly remaining exactly where they were. She felt like ripping the shirt off him. That this kind of feeling was completely out of character for her only whispered mildly along the perimeters of her mind. Center stage was frustration.

"What are they, glued in place?" A slash of accusation creased her brow.

She looked adorable stymied. Cade laughed softly at her exuberance, all the while struggling to hold his own mounting excitement in check.

"It's done with mirrors," he murmured. With effort, he squelched the impulse to help, preferring the feel of her fingers against his chest as she struggled to undress him herself.

"Well, if they don't start cooperating," she warned, "they're going to be broken mirrors very soon."

He'd known she'd be like this. In his heart, he'd known that she would be all flame and passion. That if he scratched the surface, this fiery woman would leap out.

Just seeing her in the throes of passion ignited that small part of him that was still dormant, causing it to burst into flame.

Now there were no safeguards left, no tiny islands floating in an endless sea of fire on which to seek escape. There was no escape from what he was feeling.

He wanted her.

It had been years since he'd felt like this. Years since he'd even looked at a woman. He'd been so hollow inside after losing Elaine and then Darin, he'd been certain that there was nothing there left to feel. Nothing left that he *could* feel.

He'd been wrong.

Burying his hands in the wild tangle of her hair, Cade cupped the back of Mac's neck and brought his mouth down to hers. Devouring it. Becoming something he'd never been before. A man consumed with and by desire. The agony was wonderful.

The rest happened in such a blur, it was difficult later to relate what transpired to the image he'd had of himself. Like two pieces of a puzzle that had been suddenly altered, the image was no longer complete. The pieces no longer fit.

The closer he came to having McKayla, the farther away he journeyed from the man he knew himself to be. Calm, sedate, reasonable. Driven not by emotions but by smooth, careful logic. There was nothing logical about this. None of it made any sense, except in the most unreasonable of ways.

It didn't matter.

Nothing mattered as long as he could be with her like this. As long as he could feast on her body, drink from her lips and glory in the very essence of her.

The remainder of his clothing, and hers, matted on the shining, newly installed kitchen floor in a tangle he could only hope would soon be imitated by them.

Arms woven around one another, lips sealed, they sank to the floor by silent agreement. Cade heard himself groaning in raw pleasure as he felt Mac's hands sliding along his bare skin, skimming, touching, exploring. Owning every place she touched.

Owning. Owning him.

The realization, or fragment as it were, shook him down to his very core. It would have sent him fleeing, seeking escape if he'd been able to hold on to the thought.

But he couldn't.

All he could hold on to, all he wanted to hold on to, was her. And what she was doing to him.

His mouth grazed Mac's chin as his teeth lightly nipped at her. Then, taking a better hold of her lower lip, he drew it in and suckled. Thousands of threads of pleasure went shooting throughout her body, leaving no place untouched.

Unable to remain still, she twisted beneath him. Her tongue darted out and met Cade's, sending electrical currents out to singe the threads.

Grasping her by the waist before Mac managed to maneuver over him and straddle him, Cade swung around, neatly reversing their positions. He pressed her back against the floor, his fingers woven through hers and holding them aloft, his mouth beginning a torturous journey down along the length of her creamy skin. Teasing, heating, moistening. And leaving her a mass of heaving, quivering flesh when he finally reached his goal.

With quick, sharp movements, his tongue darted in and out between her inner thighs.

She arched in spasmodic response, her eyes flying open as sudden, sharp surprise clutched her in its palm. She peaked the instant his tongue found her core. Explosions racked her body with sweet, agonizing pleasure.

Ragged breath sucked back into her lungs as her fingers came in contact with air, searching for him. Needing him. Needing to pull Cade into this circle of fire before she was too exhausted to hold on to him.

But Cade remained where he was, enjoying not the power he had over her, but the sight of her reactions. Her reactions to him.

But rather than a captor, he found himself a captive

of the woman he was pleasuring. A prisoner of her desires. And his own.

Unable to hold back any longer, he slowly drew the length of his body up along hers, hardening more with each brush. Restraint was quickly breaking through all the steely bands that held it in place.

As he was poised over her, his eyes took hers before he came to her. Before their bodies sealed together in mute promise and silent surrender.

He heard her sudden gasp, tasted it in his mouth the same moment he felt the physical resistance to his initial thrust. It was his turn to be enveloped in surprise. He would have retreated if it were up to him.

But it wasn't. The last thin thread of control was wrenched from his hands as McKayla grasped hold of his shoulders and held him to her, arching her back so that her hips thrust toward his. With a soft whimper that turned into a guttural moan, she wrapped her legs around him and melded with his body.

There was no choice.

There was only the crest and the journey to get there. And when they'd reached it, the sweetness that drenched him rained down on her as well.

Spent, he felt euphoria descend, blanket and then dissolve away in lightning speed. Even as he lay there, too tired to move, feeling her heart pounding wildly beneath his, guilt came to claim him. To clamp shackles over his wrists and ankles and hold him fast.

He shouldn't have allowed this to happen. Not after he'd realized—

Balancing himself on his elbows, he drew back from Mac so that he could look at her. His hands framed her face as he looked for the blame he was certain would be in her eyes.

What he saw first was the imprint his mouth had left on hers. The lines of her lips were blurred beyond recognition.

Damn it, he wouldn't have thought—

But she was over twenty-one…over twenty-five. How was he supposed to have known?

There were things Mac couldn't read in his eyes, but the turmoil was easy enough to make out. Apprehension stole over her, wearing very heavy, steel-tipped boots. "What?"

"Why didn't you tell me?"

Something froze inside of her as her heart scurried for high ground. For shelter it couldn't find. "Tell you what?"

"Don't play dumb, McKayla." Sitting up, his eyes cut small holes in her. "You're not dumb and pretending doesn't become you. Why didn't you tell me you were…that you'd never…"

His voice trailed off, strangled by anger, by frustration and by a pervasive helplessness that he'd destroyed something precious because of his own lack of restraint.

She struggled to maintain her dignity, to keep the tears that were suddenly, inexplicably forming from falling.

"Tell you what?" she demanded hotly. "That I'd never met a man before that I wanted to be with?" Hadn't he been listening to her? "I told you that."

Shaking his head, damning his soul, he dragged a hand impatiently through his hair. How did he make this right? You couldn't backtrack over something like this. She'd been a virgin, damn it, and he'd taken her like a rutting beast. He'd robbed her of her first time, and there was no way he could make that up to her.

"No, you said there'd never been anyone you'd ever loved."

She stared at him. "Well?" she demanded. "What did that mean to you? Did you think I was the type who slept with every breathing male I came across?"

"No, but—these days, well—" In all his life, his tongue had never felt so tangled before. His thoughts never so jumbled.

And then Mac suddenly understood what the problem was. With cool dignity cloaking her body, she gathered her clothes to her and rose to her feet, looking down at him coldly. "Don't worry, Cade, you don't have to feel obligated to me."

"Obligated?" He jumped to his feet, seemingly oblivious to his own naked state. "Damn it, McKayla, I feel guilty."

"Guilty? For what?" The demand was hot on her lips. He wasn't making any sense. But he *was* making her hot again. Try as she might, she couldn't block out the sight of his nude body standing right before her. "For giving me pleasure? For turning everything on its side and making the whole world fade away in a huge ball of fire?"

She was twisting things, absolving Cade of the blame that was his. He couldn't just lightly shrug what had happened away. "For not realizing that I was the first."

She raised her chin defensively. "And if you'd known? Would it have stopped you?"

He honestly didn't know. He would have liked to think that he had enough self-restraint, enough decency to walk away and leave her intact, but he honestly didn't know.

Cade pressed his lips together, searching his soul and still not coming up with an answer. "It might have."

"Liar. You wanted me." A touch of a smug smile lifted the corners of her mouth, cooling her anger. "I could see it in your eyes just then. And I can see it now."

Damn her, she was right. Cade had wanted her. Still wanted her. But that didn't make it right, didn't blot out the guilt.

"Wanting has nothing to do with it."

He was wrong, didn't he see that? Mac thought. "It has *everything* to do with it." For a second, her voice softened. "Don't overthink this, Cade." And then her resolve kicked in again. "You don't owe me anything for what just happened here—except maybe the courtesy to have let me enjoy it a few minutes after it was over instead of suddenly launching into an attack."

She still didn't understand, did she? "I'm not attacking you, damn it," Cade said.

"Well, it certainly feels that way from where I'm standing." The defensive edge was back in Mac's voice, in her soul.

Without realizing it, he took hold of her shoulders, not knowing if he was going to shake her, or hug her. Wanting to do both.

"It shouldn't. I'm attacking me. I shouldn't have done that to you."

"To me?" He couldn't have said anything more inflammatory to her if he'd tried. Mac jerked out of his grasp. "Mister, I was under the impression that we were in this thing together. That we were 'doing it' to each other."

Her eyes narrowed as she steeled herself off for the piercing stab of truth. As far as she could see, there was only one reason for his regretting what just happened between them.

"Was I that bad at it?"

Cade stared at her face. How could she even think that? "No, you were that good." She was getting him completely confused. With effort, Cade tried to focus. "But I still shouldn't have—"

"Shouldn't have what? Shouldn't have made me happy? Shouldn't have made me feel wonderful?" Mac fairly shouted the words at him. "Sorry, too late." Rather than rush into her clothes, she held them against her. With as much dignity as she could muster, given the situation, she turned her back and began to walk away to her room. "But like I said, I won't hold you to it."

"McKayla—"

She blinked back tears, afraid that they were going to spill out. "Go away."

"I'm sorry."

The words stopped her. Just long enough for Cade to cross to her and turn her around again to face him. Mac raised her chin. "I told you to go away." A tiny bit of a smile began to surface. "Now I'm going to have to kill you."

One by one, Cade took the clothes she was holding away from her and dropped them on the floor again until her arms were empty. And ready for him. "I'd rather you made love with me again."

Mac sighed dramatically as her heart sped up its beat again. "Well, if I have to, I have to." As he gathered her to him, she wound her arms around his neck. She hadn't a clue as to where she stood with him. But they weren't back to square one, which was all that mattered. "It's a dirty job, but I guess someone has to do it."

He lowered his mouth to hers. "Your spirit of altruism overwhelms me."

Her eyes began to close as anticipation reentered the picture again, this time its repertoire fully stocked. She knew exactly what she was anticipating, and she could hardly wait.

"As long as you know."

Chapter 12

"This isn't going to work, you know." Cade's words were meant for himself as much as for her.

Long after the euphoria from their night of lovemaking had settled into a peaceful haze, he'd wrestled with the righteous need to be honest with her.

Cade had never been one to let things just drift, unspoken and unresolved, when it was his to fix, or set right.

He kissed Mac's forehead gently, his arm still wrapped around her shoulders, holding her to him as the haze of half-broken sleep hung around them like a tattered nylon curtain. A bittersweet sadness whispered through him even as he struggled to hold on.

"'Work'?" Mac asked, raising herself up on her elbow to look at him.

Her hair, a flurry of auburn clouds, hung just over her breast, tempting his fingers and his soul. He gave in just a little, combing his fingertips through silky strands for just a moment. Lightly skimming her flesh and exciting himself even as he attempted to block the sensation.

He smiled into her eyes and wished things were different. But they weren't. He had to remember that, even though just the sight of her right now made his heart race.

"Something happened here that shouldn't have."

The simple sentence wrapped steel bands around Mac's heart and squeezed hard. And hurt.

"Regrets already? I thought I was the one who was supposed to have them, not you." Like a knocked-down fighter springing to her feet and ready to go at it again, Mac raised her chin in a challenge. "Or is that too old-fashioned?"

Cade couldn't make himself stop touching her face, even though he knew he should. For his own sanity if not for hers. "The only regret I have, McKayla, is that I'll hurt you."

Something softened inside her. The imaginary raised boxing gloves lowered. She believed him. "You're mixing tenses."

The soft laugh was rooted in truth and sadness. "Tenses aren't the only thing that's being mixed." Cade drew her to him even as he knew he should be moving her aside. The feel of her smooth body against his chest warmed him in a hundred ways he hadn't been warmed for a very long time. "McKayla, the driving force in my life is finding my son."

Her eyes were wide and understanding as she looked at him. "I know that."

She heard the words, he thought, but she still didn't

understand. "Up until last night, there hasn't been anything else in my life but that."

It was foolish to feel herself grow still, foolish for words to mean so much when their time together had been so infinitesimally short. And yet, Mac felt as if something huge was riding on what he said next. She held her breath. "And now?"

"And now there still won't be anything else," he said, looking into her eyes for a sign that she understood. "There *can't* be. It's not fair to bring you into something like that. To make you stand in the background—"

Mac had no intention of standing in the background. It wasn't her way. She wanted to help him, just as he was helping her. That was what caring was all about. It always had been. And they both knew this wasn't permanent. The fact that it wasn't was what gave her the strength, the courage to press on.

She brushed her lips over his. "Why don't you let me decide what's fair?"

Cade shook his head. "I can't decide anything if you're going to do that."

She smiled at the compliment. It would have been an easy thing to get accustomed to, but the risks attached to it, for her, were far too great.

"I'm not asking for first place, Cade. I'm not asking for anything at all, except maybe a little island of time." She kissed him again. "Okay?"

No demands, no strings. It seemed like the perfect arrangement to Cade. A slow grin emerged. "You drive a hell of an argument."

She pretended to toss her head proudly. "First in my debating team."

The grin turned into a laugh just as he was about to press a kiss to her shoulder. "Why doesn't that surprise me?"

Nothing about this woman, Cade realized, would really surprise him. By her very existence, she was the definition of surprise. He'd thought of her as earthy, worldly, yet she was a virgin. She'd made it clear that being in charge was something she was accustomed to, yet she was apparently content to let this thing between them, whatever it was, just float.

A complete surprise, through and through.

He reached for her, wanting to pleasure her and himself again, before the dream was over.

Like cold water suddenly falling from the sky, the shrill ring doused the rising flame between them, galvanizing their attention to the telephone immediately. Lovemaking took a back seat.

Rolling over in the bed, Mac clamped her hand over the receiver first. Her heart was hammering hard as she pulled it to her. "Hello?"

"Mrs. Sinclair?" The doctor's rich, kindly voice filled her ear.

Two hands now on the receiver, she scooted up on the bed. "Yes." Her eyes meeting Cade's, she nodded at the question she saw there.

"This is Dr. Lambert," the man said unnecessarily. "I think I might have some good news for you."

"What is it?" She didn't have to fake the slight tremor in her voice. Mac felt on the verge of a bonanza.

"My lawyer, Phillip Taylor, just informed me that he's free this evening if you and your husband would still like to—"

She had no idea if the doctor was being cautious or coy, or simply enjoying his role as benevolent benefactor. But it wasn't her job to analyze him.

Knowing Lambert expected a show of emotion, she didn't disappoint him. The word *yes* tumbled out breathlessly. She placed a gentling hand on Cade's as he gripped her shoulder in silent query. She didn't even dare to look at him.

"My husband and I would *love* to meet with you and Mr. Taylor. Anyplace, anytime. Oh, Doctor, you have no idea how long I've waited—" She paused, drawing in air as if her throat was closed off by emotion.

"I know, my dear, I know," Lambert assured her warmly. "And I understand. Believe me, the waiting may be over with very soon."

He said "may," she thought. Not will, but may. The man was being very cautious. She pulled out the stops on her performance. "Just name the time and place."

Lambert began giving her the name of a restaurant. Mac looked around for something to write with.

"Wait, wait—there's never a pencil when you need one." She yanked open the nightstand drawer and felt around inside. To her surprise, she came in contact with a pen and small yellow pad. Apparently the word *furnished* was carried out to the nth degree, she thought gratefully. "Got it!" She scribbled quickly. "The Blue Quail, eight o'clock." She felt more than saw Cade looking over her shoulder at the pad. "Reservations will be in your name?"

"No, my dear," Lambert corrected her. "They'll be in yours."

Why was there this uneasy feeling when he said that? "Wonderful." Mac laid down the pen. "Just as long as we connect, it doesn't matter whose name the reservations are under. We'll see you then."

Agreeing, the doctor rang off.

But it did matter, she thought, as she hung up. Lambert wouldn't have made the reservations in their name if it didn't. Why?

Cade glanced at his watch. It was barely eight. The doctor apparently kept early hours. Or he was anxious to get rid of his latest acquisition. His guess was the latter.

"Well?" he pressed, looking at Mac. "Is the meeting for tonight?"

She nodded slowly. "The reservation is in our name. Is that rather strange?"

"The less that points to him, the better. Men like Lambert don't like loose ends, or fingers pointing at them. They clean up before and after themselves."

Pulling the light blanket up to cover herself, she studied Cade's face thoughtfully. "You've dealt with people like Lambert before?"

"You mean people who ran a black-market ring?" She nodded. "No, I haven't, but I'm familiar with the type. A predator who preys on people's emotional neediness."

"He sounds so sincere—" She shook her head. How many unsuspecting people had he duped? How many went to bed each night, blessing the fact that their paths had crossed the doctor's? And how many more lives were going to be shattered by the time this was over?

"Camouflage," Cade assured her.

Her mind was already moving forward to the next problem. "How do we get word to Redhawk?"

Why did that blanket look so enticing wrapped around her? And what was wrong with him? He was the most single-minded man he knew, able to keep his mind focused no matter what.

Obviously, McKayla Dellaventura was a completely new type of "what."

Because he needed to focus, he answered her question. "We go out to buy a bottle of champagne to celebrate the possible expansion of our family by one. And while I'm paying for the purchase, and hopefully keeping Lambert's paid flunky occupied, you excuse yourself to use the nearby ladies' room—and a public telephone."

"Sounds like a plan." She was already scrambling off the bed, ready to get ready.

"One that isn't going to go into action for at least a couple of hours." He caught her hand before she got very far.

"Why?" She turned to look at him. "What did you have in mind?"

"Liquor stores don't open until ten," he pointed out.

Mac nodded, taking this information in. She hadn't thought of that. That gave them some time to kill. She didn't like the idea of the minutes dragging by. "In the mood for breakfast?"

Heaven help him, Cade hardly recognized himself as he drew her back to the bed. "No, not breakfast." He watched her raise an eyebrow he suddenly found delectable. "Let me show you what I am in the mood for."

* * *

The mission, when they finally got themselves out of Cade's bedroom and to the store, was executed with great success. While Cade engaged the store clerk in a lengthy debate over the merits of several bottles of champagne, Mac slipped out to call Redhawk. She quickly informed him of the meeting. Pleased with herself and the feeling that they had managed to put one over on the man tailing their every move, Mac continued to mentally rehearse the meeting to come.

It wasn't until after several hours of torturous, inert waiting, with a for-the-most-part unwatched movie flickering on one of the television's cable channels, that Mac realized that she had overlooked something very basic.

Swinging around to look at Cade, she cried, "Oh, God."

Instantly alert, his eyes swept over the immediate area as he took her hand. "What?"

She groaned, then looked at the clock. There was no time to rush out and remedy this. The doctor was expecting them soon. "I have nothing to wear."

She looked so serious, it was all Cade could do not to choke on his laughter. "*Now* you're getting typical on me?"

Frustrated, she doubled her fist and punched his arm for lack of any other handy target. "I'm serious. I came prepared for shadowing, grabbing and running, not for slinking."

Though he was looking at her now, he was thinking of the way she'd looked just a few short hours ago. "You do that pretty well without the trappings of any special clothing."

Or any clothing at all, he added silently.

Mac stopped in her tracks and cocked her head to one side, studying him. "Is that a compliment?"

The smile that took over was a tad lopsided. "Yeah, I guess it is."

"Well, then thank you." Mac pressed a kiss to his temple. And found herself wanting to continue and to give him more. She silently upbraided herself for her lack of control. That had never happened before. She was always the soul of control. Over herself and others. "And what do you mean, now I'm getting typical on you?" she asked. "Just when was I atypical?"

"Right up until now. Everything about you is different from the kind of woman I'm used to."

Coy was something she had no patience with. So were games. So it was with complete surprise that she heard herself asking, "Good different or bad different?"

Cade winked mysteriously as he walked into the kitchen, but she could have sworn there was a smile tugging on his lips. "Let's just leave it at different."

Opening the refrigerator, he looked in and debated uncorking the bottle they'd bought. She looked as if she could use a little something to help steady her nerves. But it might make things worse, he decided. Cade let the door close and focused on her initial lament. "By the way, have you looked in the closet?"

The question struck Mac as odd. But she'd already picked up the fact that Cade didn't ask questions without a reason. "Why? Should I?"

He nodded. "Redhawk's very thorough, even un-officially. There's an entire wardrobe in there. I'm sure you'll find something suitable to wear for din-ner."

"An entire wardrobe?" She sincerely doubted that. Most men had no concept what that meant. To them, an entire wardrobe was two matching outfits. Three on the outside. "Whose?"

"Caitlin's." Cade had checked it out himself ear-lier. To his eye, it appeared that Caitlin and McKayla were about the same size. "Redhawk's wife," he elaborated when McKayla still looked confused.

"I'd better hustle if we want to make this place on time." With that, she hurried up the small, winding staircase to the room she'd taken over as her own.

Cade followed her up, enjoying the view, telling himself he had no right to let his mind wander this way. He needed to be sharp, to focus. To look for possible slipups on their part as well as on the doc-tor's or Taylor's.

Entering his room, Cade went straight to the closet. Luckily, he was around the same build as the detec-tive. Something else they had in common, he mused, beyond their Native American heritage. Of course, he was only one-quarter Cherokee while Gray was one-half Navajo, on his mother's side.

He took out the light gray suit and found a shirt in the bureau. Hunter green. The man thought of every-thing, he thought in admiration.

Cade was even more convinced of Redhawk's fore-sight when he walked out of his bedroom a few minutes later. Mac was already in the living room, ready. He was no longer surprised by her speed. What caught him off guard was what she was wearing. A long-sleeved hunter green dress that hugged all her curves like a familiar lover.

They matched, he noted, the thought telegraphing itself to him in a delayed relay.

"Nice," he managed to murmur.

The next moment he almost swallowed his tongue as Mac turned around for him in a full circle. It was obvious that the designer had chosen to cut a few corners, specifically that portion of her dress that went from her neck to her waist. Her back was completely bare and completely enticing.

He couldn't find his voice without clearing his throat. "Isn't that a little drafty?"

The understatement amused her. "I thought that, too, but I figure I can always find something to drape over me." Turning around to face him, she smiled invitingly. But just as Cade moved to slip his arm around her shoulders, Mac threw a white cashmere wrap over them. Her eyes teased him as she realized that she was flirting with him. It was an entirely new experience for her. "Isn't it gorgeous?" She slid her fingers along the material. "I almost feel sinful, wearing this."

He tried not to picture her wearing *only* that and succeeded marginally.

"It looks like something his mother might have made," he commented. "She's a full-blooded Navajo."

Mac held out one arm to inspect the work more closely. The wrap was heavily fringed and exquisitely embroidered just along the ends. "Well, she certainly does beautiful work."

"Yes, it is beautiful," he agreed, slipping his arm around her and escorting her out the door. Almost as beautiful as the woman wearing it.

They had little trouble finding the restaurant. Located on a long boulevard that was home to a number of restaurants on both sides, the Blue Quail, with its rich history and fine tradition dating back over a hundred years, stood out like a regal dowager looking out benevolently on younger upstarts that were destined to come and go without leaving a mark.

A parking attendant strode toward them before Cade had a chance to shut off the engine. He was driving a Mercedes now, having traded in the less-expensive model he'd rented in order to perpetuate the aura of money to burn.

Mac slid out on her side as the attendant held her door open for her. She could get used to this, she thought. More than that, she could get used to being with Cade.

Warning signals went off in her head. It was dangerous to let herself even speculate along those lines.

As Cade took her arm to enter the restaurant, she inclined her head toward his. "Lambert certainly knows how to live."

"Yeah." Cade's mouth was grim. "The baby-selling business must be very lucrative."

The maître d' raised a brow ever so slightly at their entrance, guarding a red velvet rope and the passage into the dining hall solicitously.

"Sinclair, party of four," Cade told him.

"Ah, yes, I believe the other two gentlemen have already arrived." With a subdued movement, the slender man lifted the rope, picked up two menus and led them to a secluded table for four.

Had this been England, Mac thought, at first sight the two dignified-looking men sitting at their table would have been thought to belong to the aristocracy of old. They both had the air of refined respectability about them. Mac couldn't help wondering if there'd been some kind of a mix-up. Maybe they weren't really involved.

Lambert was on his feet the moment he saw them approach. The other man, Taylor, echoed his movement, smiling benevolently. The doctor's smile was wider as he took her hand in both of his in welcome. "Mrs. Sinclair, you do look stunning."

And he looked like the big, bad wolf, about to eat a sacrificial lamb for dinner, Cade thought. In a move that was purely unconscious on his part, Cade closed a proprietary arm around Mac's waist. The momentary feel of bare skin against his hand sent thoughts flying through his mind that had absolutely nothing to do with why they were here. But everything to do with his possessive reflex.

"*Stunned* is more like it," she confessed as the maître d' helped her with her chair. Her eyes never left Lambert's face. "My head is still reeling. I had no idea that you would work so fast."

"Permit me to introduce Phillip Taylor." The lawyer, somewhat younger-looking than Lambert, leaned over to first shake hands with Cade, then with Mac as Lambert made the necessary introductions. Folding his hands before him, he resumed his conversation with Mac. "Ordinarily, we don't move nearly this quickly, but times have been hard on several of the young women I know. Since you are so eager to adopt, I thought I would just get the preliminary ball rolling.'' The smile was meant to put them at their ease. He'd had many years of practice with skittish patients and he did his job, he liked to think, well. It was second nature to him. ''Do you have any preferences?'' He looked from husband to wife, knowing in most instances, it was the woman who made the decision. ''Boy, girl? Infant, toddler?''

''Or perhaps an older child?'' Taylor interjected quietly.

Cade looked at him with interest. It was a struggle to smother the loathing he felt and keep it from registering on his face. ''You place older children?''

''By older, I meant four, five, possibly six,'' Taylor clarified. With two fingertips, he smoothed down a pencil-thin mustache that was iron gray and half a shade darker than his hair. He sighed, looking into his glass. ''These are very difficult times for some people.'' His eyes shifted to Mac. ''A little like that opening line by Charles Dickens.''

'' 'It was the best of times, it was the worst of times'?'' Mac suggested.

He nodded. His eyes washed over her and lingered with proper approval. ''That's the one. Beautiful and intelligent.'' Taylor raised his glass to Cade. ''Some men have all the luck.''

In a move that came all too naturally, Cade placed his hand over McKayla's on the table. ''Not all, but pretty close to it.''

Lambert nodded knowingly. His smile was kind, understanding and sympathetic. ''And by that you mean because you don't have a son to carry on your name.''

Even the simple words cut deep. He had to keep his feelings at bay. ''Actually, I was thinking more along the lines of a daughter.''

Mac caught the look of pain that passed fleetingly over Cade's face and covered for him quickly, drawing attention away. ''My husband doesn't have an ego problem. He'd much rather have a daughter than a son.''

''And you, my dear?'' Lambert pressed. ''What would you much rather have?''

She shook her head, not wanting to say a single word that might tip either man off that they were anything but legitimately seeking a child to adopt. ''I don't care if it's either.''

''As long as it's healthy—'' Taylor began to parrot. He'd heard the phrase ad nauseum.

''As long as I can share my heart with him or her,'' Mac interjected.

The two older men exchanged looks, two residents of an exclusive men's club sharing a mutual confidence that needed no words. Mac mentally held her breath.

Taylor spoke first. ''You are a rare woman indeed, Mrs. Sinclair.''

''Julia, please,'' Mac corrected him, using her alias. The faster they got the men to feel completely in control and at ease, the faster this would progress.

''Julia, then. Let's eat, shall we?'' Signaling an intermission to the discussion, Taylor opened his menu. He barely looked at the page. Mac had a feeling that he knew what was written there by heart. ''And then we can discuss the particulars regarding the adoption.''

Adrenaline shot through her as she watched the men calmly regard their menus. It was all she could do to keep from leaping over the table, wrapping her hands around Taylor's thin throat and demanding to know where her niece was.

And wouldn't that play well? she mocked herself.

So instead, with Cade beside her, emotionally holding her hand and acting as a calming influence, Mac went through the motions of ordering a very light meal. After having made love with Cade, she'd been famished. Now she had absolutely no appetite to speak of. There was only a huge knot in the pit of her stomach. A knot that wouldn't allow her to eat.

When it arrived, Mac picked at her food, trying valiantly to hold up her end of the small talk. It was a losing battle. All she could think of was Heather. Where was she? Was she all right? Was she frightened? Would they really find her, or was this all just a futile charade?

Lambert looked reprovingly at her plate. ''Why, Julia, you're not eating. What sort of example will you set for your child if you don't eat healthily?''

''There'll be plenty of opportunity to set a good example once I have a child.'' She pasted a smile on her face, the nervous mother-to-be. Giving up, she retired her fork on a battlefield of once carefully arranged salad. ''I'm sorry, Dr. Lambert. I feel as if we're so close now.'' A flush borne of suppressed anger, not embarrassment, crept over her cheeks. ''It's like the jitters you get as a child the night before Christmas—''

"I understand perfectly," Lambert said, appearing to enjoy his role as a benevolent granter of wishes. "Well, perhaps we should stop torturing you good people and let you take a look at this." Without waiting for concurrence from his partner, Lambert produced a small collection of photographs from his pocket and placed them on the table in front of him.

Cade noted the look of muted irritation on Taylor's face. Had Lambert spoken out of turn or usurped his position?

"What is that?" Cade asked.

The wide hand lovingly stroked the pale blue cover. "Photographs of some of the children who need homes." Lambert looked directly at Mac. "Children whose mothers cannot take care of them. Noble young women who want their children to have certain opportunities. Here, feel free to look." With a small push, he moved the pictures toward Cade. "Look upon the face of your future child."

The doctor was getting carried away in his role, Cade thought as he looked at the photographs. Close-ups taken with what looked to be a portrait camera.

Heather's face was among the camera shots. Cade could feel Mac tensing ever so slightly beside him. It was his turn to run interference. To divert attention away from her, he looked at some of the others, commenting on the faces as he looked, feeling his heart tighten in empathetic anguish at each new face.

"You make it hard to pick just one," he said, continuing to look.

"I'd say take two—" Taylor laughed "—but they don't come any cheaper that way, I'm afraid. For each child you see there, there is a mother who has expenses that need to be taken care of. In some cases, long, outstanding hospital bills—'' He stopped abruptly as he saw the strange expression on Cade's face. ''Is something the matter, Mr. Sinclair?''

Cade barely heard the question. His breath had stopped and there was a strange buzzing in his head. He was staring down at a little boy's photograph.

At Darin's photograph.

Chapter 13

Mac had never actually seen a photograph of Darin Townsend, had no idea what Cade's son looked like. But some inner instinct told her that the child's face who was causing Cade to momentarily freeze had to be that of his own son. She knew it with a certainty that was unshakable.

Her mind scrambling, she searched for a way to divert attention away from Cade until he got himself completely under control.

The ladies' room.

Reaching for her clutch purse, she fanned herself with it as she let out a large breath. She flashed the two men an apologetic smile.

"If you gentlemen will excuse me for a moment, I'm afraid all this—" she indicated the opened album "—has made me very emotional. I need a moment to collect myself." Rising to her feet, she told Cade, "I'll be in the ladies' room."

But it was Lambert who spoke instead of Cade. "Is there anything I can—"

No, but you will, she silently promised him with a vengeance. Out loud, she was the portrait of geniality. "No, thank you. Just a little cold water on my neck and wrists should sufficiently revive me. I can't tell you how excited this is making me."

With Mac making her way to the rest rooms, Lambert looked thoughtfully at Cade scrutinizing the photograph in front of him.

Lambert smiled. The boy had been the start of it all. Ironic that his adoptive parents had suddenly decided to return him, saying they were not emotionally equipped to handle such a deeply saddened child.

Despite that, Lambert bore a certain amount of affection for him.

He tapped a well-manicured finger on the plastic surface covering the photograph. "I see you're struck with Jeremy."

Cade looked up then. It all felt surreal. Lambert's words, his own responses, everything. There was no other word for it except *surreal.*

"Jeremy?" Cade echoed the strange name without comprehension.

Was that what Darin answered to now? Jeremy? Cade forced himself not to look down at the photograph again, afraid that his pain would show through and give everything away.

But if he thought anything was amiss, Lambert gave no indication. Instead, he turned the book around so that the photograph was right side up for him and looked down at it. He shook his head.

"Yes, tragic the way the boy came to us. He and

his parents were in a car accident. His parents never survived. The boy has no family to speak of, but I feel rather responsible for him. His mother was my receptionist,'' he explained. ''He's exceedingly bright. You can tell by the eyes.''

Anger warred with other, equally volatile emotions. For the first time in his life, Cade felt capable of extreme violence. Lambert was talking about his son as if he were nothing more than a pet, a puppy bred for certain qualities. Was that how the abducted children were chosen, for appealing qualities that made them easy to place, easy to be rid of?

Cade struggled to keep his voice level, his tone friendly. ''Where is Jeremy now?''

''He's staying with my wife and me.'' Lambert turned the album around again so that Cade could view it easily, seeking to strike while the opportunity was there. He'd all but given up thinking of placing the boy; now there seemed a chance.

''It's a temporary arrangement that I must admit is beginning to take on permanent roots.'' He toyed with his glass, but other than his initial sip, Lambert had left the contents untouched. He never drank when he negotiated. ''I'm very fond of Jeremy, of course, but if someone were willing to give him a good home— the proper environment and that sort of thing, then I would feel as if my work was done.''

You bastard. ''What kind of money are we talking about?'' Though Cade glanced at Taylor, it was Lambert's eyes he looked directly into. He had a feeling that Lambert was the key person in this drama. ''To get the adoption moving, I mean?''

''For Jeremy?'' Thin shoulders shrugged beneath

an expertly tailored jacket. "Nominal, really." He thought for a moment. "Standard court costs, lawyer's fees. Perhaps a small reimbursement for having cared for Jeremy over the last year."

The mention of the time pulled Cade up short. "A year?"

"That's how long he's been with us."

A year. Not three. But then, Lambert could be, and undoubtedly was, lying. There was no reason to think the man would be telling the truth about this.

The boy in the photograph was not some fictional child named Jeremy, but Darin. Cade would have bet his soul on it.

Like a sympathetic uncle, Lambert leaned forward and asked in a confidential tone, "Are you interested in adopting Jeremy, perhaps? I know that you said you and Julia wanted a daughter, but believe me, Jeremy is something special."

"Yes," Cade said quietly, "I can see that he is."

He glanced toward Taylor again. For the most part, the man had been silent throughout the discussion, but the lawyer apparently was more interested in the contents of his glass than he was in the lives of the innocents who were being bandied about.

As he began to say something to Lambert, Cade became aware that someone was standing just to his side. When he looked up, he saw the waiter hovering, waiting for a break in the conversation.

"Yes?"

"Mr. Sinclair?" When Cade nodded, the man continued. "There's a phone call for you. I'm sorry, but our portable telephone is not working at the moment.

But you can take the call at the reception desk." He pointed toward the entrance.

"I'm sorry. It's probably something to do with work. I told them where I could be reached. They seem to work round the clock there." Rising, Cade hoped that the nebulous excuse would suffice.

"Think nothing of it. I'm accustomed to my work interrupting every phase of my life," Lambert said, laughing as he waved Cade on.

It had to be Redhawk calling, Cade thought as he picked up the receiver. No one else even knew he was here. He hadn't gotten in touch with his own office since he and Mac had arrived.

But when he got on the telephone, it was Mac's voice he heard.

"Are you all right?"

Stunned, he scanned the immediate area. Was she using her cell phone? And where was their ever-present shadow during all this? He just assumed that the P.I. was somewhere close by.

"McKayla? Why are you calling me?"

She stood, watching his back from the recesses of the alcove that housed both rest rooms and the bank of three telephones between them. "I'm at the pay phones right behind you." She saw him begin to look over his shoulder. That was the last thing she wanted if he was being watched. "No, don't turn around, just keep looking toward the door. I wanted to get you away from the table before Lambert started asking questions. You turned as white as fresh oatmeal." She paused for half a second, knowing that even hearing the question was going to hurt him. "Was that Darin in the album?"

"I think so." If he told her he was positive, she'd only think he was talking himself into it. There were a great many changes that occurred between three and six. But that had been Darin. He knew that as well as he knew his own name.

The significance of his words hit Mac with force. How many other families had this scum with a fatherly smile torn apart? "Let's get them."

"No, we're going to play this out. If we spring the trap too soon, some of the other people involved might escape detection. Or worse, the records might be destroyed, and then we won't be able to locate all the children that have been kidnapped in the name of the almighty dollar."

Mac moved closer to the wall, lowering her voice even more as a woman passed her on the way to the ladies' room. "What makes you think there're records?"

Cade laughed shortly. "Easy. That kind always keeps records. Call it a sort of a self-glorification." Chronicles for other people to see and be in awe of. In this case, it would be other, lesser members of the black-market ring.

They'd both been away from the table for several minutes now. He didn't want Lambert getting suspicious. "Why don't you come back from the ladies' room first, and then I'll join them at the table?"

"Okay." She began to hang up, then stopped when she heard the sound of his voice coming from the receiver, calling her name. "Yes?"

"I just wanted to thank you."

"For what?"

"For being concerned. For coming to save my tail." He'd never had a woman do that before.

"Anytime. And Cade?"

"Yeah?"

She smiled, even though he couldn't see her. "We're going to get through this."

They had no other choice. Anything else was unthinkable. "Right."

Cade set the receiver back in its cradle. Darin. He'd found Darin. After three barren years, during which it appeared as if his son had been swallowed up by the very earth, he had finally located Darin.

He'd wanted this so badly for so long, it was almost impossible to believe he was finally on the right path.

It took every fiber of his self-control not to follow through on his instincts and confront both men when he returned to the table. Confront them with the truth and demand to have his son returned before another breath was drawn.

But he knew that nothing but denials would come of that. His hands tied, he continued with the charade he had already counseled Mac to keep up. It wasn't just his son and her niece he had to think about. There were a lot of Darins and Heathers at stake here. It was a hell of a responsibility, and he knew he couldn't afford the luxury of acting on his own feelings.

But when this was over, when the names and locations of the other stolen children were found, he wanted to be closeted with Lambert and Taylor for just five minutes. Five minutes with them, his bare fists and raw emotions. To even the score for Darin and to pay them back, just a little, for what he'd gone through.

"Sorry that took so long." Cade slid back into his seat.

Lambert waved the words away. "No need to apologize. A man's work has to come first." The genial smile took them both in, coming to rest on the closed album. "So, have you made your decision yet?"

Cade exchanged glances with Mac. It was important not to arouse any undue suspicions. "We'd like to adopt the little girl." He flipped the page over to Heather's photograph. "This one."

He touched the page with the tip of his finger. He had a responsibility to Mac. She was his client and he was working this case to recover the eighteen-month-old little girl. Finding Darin was a bonus he meant to collect on once his duties were properly executed.

Lambert appeared pleased with the choice. "Excellent." He turned the book over toward him again to verify which child it was. "Lily. She is a pixie, isn't she?"

"Pixie," Mac echoed with a smile on her lips that she knew was mandatory. And then she placed her hand on Cade's arm, drawing his attention back to her. "Honey, why don't we give Lily an older brother?" As Cade turned toward her in mute surprise, Mac looked at Lambert. "Could we do that? Adopt the boy as well?"

The process was easier than talking about it. Lambert looked at her face over the rim of his glasses, appearing to scrutinize her. "You want them both?"

She nodded, her enthusiasm growing as she spoke.

"There's just something about that face that speaks to my heart. And they even look enough alike to pass for brother and sister." Her hand tightened on Cade's arm, squeezing for emphasis. "What do you say?" She couldn't read his eyes when he turned toward her. Had she overstepped? Or messed something up? "We've certainly got enough love for both. And we've waited so long..."

Taylor had finished what was, by Cade's count, his third drink. He looked a little saddened that he had nothing to raise in toast. Rallying, he lifted an imaginary goblet. "Looks like your wife's made up her mind." He laughed at his own joke before sharing it. "And we married men all know what that means."

"Tough lady to argue with," Cade agreed.

Inside, he wasn't anywhere near as calm as he appeared. He couldn't help wondering if they had overplayed their hand somehow and if the men saw through them. Or did they simply view Mac's behavior as the reaction of a woman who had just been granted her dearest wish after years of having it denied?

He looked intently at Lambert. "So, is it doable?"

"That is entirely up to you, Mr. Sinclair, but I would certainly say that I believe it is." Lambert smiled magnanimously as he turned his attention to Taylor beside him. There was just the slightest hint of disapproval in his gray eyes as they flickered over the glass. "Are you sure?"

"We're sure," Mac said firmly. She covered Cade's hand with hers, afraid to look at him. Afraid that too much could be read into their glances.

"All right, then, Phillip will see to the arrangements and give you a call tomorrow morning.'' Lambert looked at his Rolex not because he needed to know the time, but because he enjoyed looking at fine things. ''Say around ten?''

Ten.

More than twelve hours to live in limbo, Mac thought. More than twelve hours to reside on the cusp of hell. But they had no choice. For the moment, Lambert and Taylor were in the driver's seat. The additional time could be put to use, she reminded herself. They could alert Redhawk, and he finally could go to his superior with this as evidence. Once they caught the men in the art of literally ''selling'' kidnapped children, the ring could be cracked wide open. The children could be sent home.

And she could bring Heather back to Moira, the way she promised.

There was a trace of breathlessness in her voice when she told Lambert, ''We'll be counting the minutes.''

''I'm sure you will.''

Whatever else he might have had to say was swallowed up in the shrill, insistent ring of his cell phone. Excusing himself, he took it out. The genial expression on his face melted into one of resignation.

''Yes, of course. I'll be right there.'' He flipped the phone closed. A semiapologetic expression fell into place as he looked at them. ''It seems my presence is required to help welcome twins into the world. A week early, I might add.'' He sighed. In a rare show of confidence, he added, ''At times, I find that the miracle of birth is a highly overrated affair.'' He tucked the telephone away into his pocket as he rose from the table. Pausing, he looked at Cade. "You'll pick up my tab?"

Cade found the question incredibly miserly, coming from a man wearing a suit that must have cost at least four hundred dollars and a Rolex watch.

"Consider it done." Cade looked at Taylor. "Yours, too, of course." The bar tab alone would probably be costly, he mused. But it was a small-enough price to pay, considering what was at stake.

Taylor merely nodded his thanks. Apparently becoming aware of Lambert's prolonged scrutiny, his expression was infused with just a whisper of resentment.

"Maybe I had better call it a night as well. I'll get back to you in the morning," he promised Cade and Mac as he rose to his feet.

Hands were shaken, promises made. Mac and Cade remained at the table as the two men left. Mac held her breath, watching them go. After she was sure they had departed, Mac squeezed Cade's hand. She could hardly believe it.

"It's happening. We're going to get them back," she whispered, looking at him. For a man who was finally in sight of his goal, he looked oddly subdued. Was there something he hadn't told her, or was this just his reticent way? "Aren't you excited?"

He was afraid to be excited, Cade realized. "Once I have Darin in my arms again, there'll be time enough to be excited."

He'd spent too long in this abyss to be certain that he was climbing out again, even if there appeared to be proof that he was. Things didn't always turn out the way they were supposed to. Plans went awry.

They fell apart. He didn't want to begin rejoicing just yet. He couldn't put up with the disappointment after that.

"Do you think they suspect us?"

He thought before answering. "No, but it doesn't hurt to be cautious."

Mac had been cautious all her life when it came to certain things. Cautious because she was afraid of falling on her face. Of becoming dependent on something that wasn't dependable. She knew all about caution. And the pitfalls it brought with it.

"Yes, it does. Sometimes," she murmured, almost more to herself than to him. "Sometimes being cautious costs you a great deal, and what there is after that hurts twice as much." Because what there is after that is loneliness, she thought.

But if she was cautious when it came to giving her heart away, Mac certainly wasn't when it came to believing that they were merely hours away from finding Heather.

The rush she felt wouldn't abate. She found that it was more than a little difficult to get control over the surging that kept insisting on seizing her body, running madly from corner to corner as it filled in all the spaces. In light of Cade's subdued reaction, she was vainly attempting to maintain control.

It was a losing battle.

Leaving the restaurant shortly after Lambert and Taylor's exit, Cade and Mac drove back to the condo. Unable to restrain herself, Mac kept up a steady stream of conversation. It was interrupted only on occasion by Cade, and then only with a noise rather than a word.

By the time they pulled into their parking space, Mac didn't think she could take Cade's somber mood any longer, not without an explanation.

Getting out, she swung the door shut behind her. "Do you want to tell me what's eating at you?"

He hit the combination lock on the door, scrambling the code for the keyless entry. "Nothing."

Nothing, her foot. "'Nothing' is what you've said for the last ten miles."

Cade looked at her, mild surprise creasing his forehead. "I answered you."

She almost laughed out loud. "Grunting is only considered a language by cave dwellers." And then the reason for his reluctance hit her. "Are you afraid that you're wrong, that it's not him?" Cade had seemed so sure when she'd spoken to him in the restaurant.

Cade thought of the face in the photograph. His stomach tightened. "No, it's Darin, all right. He looks just like his mother. And just like Megan's projection." He considered dropping it. There was no reason to share his feelings with this woman. But Cade heard himself doing it nonetheless. "What I'm afraid of is that at the last minute, this is all going to fall apart and I'll be back to square one."

So that was it. In her heart, Mac had suspected something like this. "It's not going to fall apart," she insisted softly. She followed Cade to the front door and waited as he put in the key.

"We'll get him back."

She used the term *we* as if they were a team, like

he and Megan were. And like Sam, Cade thought. But they weren't. She wasn't. She was a client, and the sooner he started remembering that, the better off they would all be. "Darin isn't your concern."

Mac's eyes held his. She wondered if he truly believed that, if he thought she could just walk away after what they'd just been through. "Yeah, he is. If we find Heather, then I'll owe you."

"The bill will be in the mail."

The remark stung. She walked into the house. "More than money can ever pay." Mac turned around as he flipped the locks into place on the door. "And if I help you find Darin, then the debt will be paid."

"Then I'll owe you," he pointed out.

"One debt will absolve the other," she assured him. She looked around the neatly ordered condo, feeling restless and antsy. Mac took a deep breath. The feeling only intensified. "So what do we do now?"

There was nothing they could do. Cade had already called Redhawk before they'd left the restaurant, alerting him to what had happened. Redhawk had things to do, but they didn't. They were in the pending mode. "We wait."

Mac didn't want to wait, she wanted to jump into action. To go to Lambert's house and demand the release of her niece and his son. "Part of me—"

Cade read her thoughts in her eyes. "Yes, I know. Me, too."

They were on the same page, Mac realized, the same wavelength. It amazed her how alike they could be.

"I'm not going to be able to sleep tonight," Mac confessed. She glanced at the television set. It was the off month, just before the TV sweeps began. Programs were into reruns. Staring at reruns held no appeal to her. She thought about what she'd done in college on the eve of killer finals. "How are you at card games?"

"All I know is poker."

The word evoked a huge grin from her. A man after her own heart. "Funny you should say that, it's my favorite card game."

Cade had trouble envisioning her playing poker. He'd always equated it with something men did in smoky rooms with the smell of beer occasionally piercing the cigar-infested cloud.

"I pictured you as more of the cerebral type. Bridge, something like that."

Bridge had always moved too slowly to satisfy her. Mac liked something with motion.

"Shows you can never judge a book by its cover." Standing on her toes, she opened the kitchen cupboards and rummaged around for something to use. She came up with a very poor selection. "You want to play for matchsticks, paper clips or gumdrops?"

Her back was to him. All of her back, with nothing else in the way. Poker became the furthest thing from Cade's mind. "I think I have something a great deal sweeter in mind than gumdrops."

Chapter 14

With each pass of his hands, the tension of the day was smoothed away a little more. Pushed further and further back until it was less than an infinitesimal dot looming somewhere on the horizon. Not forgotten, but for the moment, ignored.

And with every movement of his hands, Cade evoked another kind of tension, another sort of anticipation, from deep within Mac's soul. One that healed rather than destroyed. One that ultimately soothed rather than agitated.

Like a traveler at the end of a thousand-mile journey, Mac rushed toward the light that burned brightly for her in the window, welcoming her home. Welcoming her to a place that she had not understood, until this very moment, actually existed. She embraced it and him with open arms and with no reservations.

At least for now.

Turning in the comforting circle formed by Cade's arms, Mac surrendered completely to the sensations that so swiftly laid claim to her. Gave herself up to the man who made her feel so many things, so many joys, anticipations and a host of other, equally passionate emotions she had neither the time nor ability to sort out yet. All she knew was that having them made her feel invulnerable. Capable of anything.

Of everything.

This had to be what love was like, she realized. The thought would have shaken her down to her very shoes had she been able to think clearly. But thinking was not a priority, only feeling was.

The sound of her breathing, growing more audible with each movement he made, excited Cade beyond his own comprehension. It was as if every breath she took ended in his own lungs, in his own body. Fueling, not sating, the desire that blossomed and grew so quickly.

He wanted to go fast, to take her and make wild, exquisite love before doubts and fears caught up to him, making him back away.

He wanted to go slow, so that every movement, every breath, was firmly and indelibly imprinted on his brain. So that it would last a lifetime. As this would not. He'd had happiness snatched out of his hands too many times to believe that it would last for more than a very fleeting juncture in time. But memories, memories could last for as long as he had breath in his body.

And he was making memories with her now.

Coaxed by his hands, the green dress shimmied

down away from her shoulders ever so slowly. The silver threads that were shot through it caught the light, giving it warm life and throwing it back at him.

As if he needed that to catch his attention.

The smile on his lips did not begin to give expression to the awe, to the wonder he felt at being the first man to make love with this woman. How could she have gone so many years and never had someone worship her body with his hands the way he was doing now? How could she have walked the earth, lived her life, and not had men begging to do what he was doing now?

The implications that went hand in hand with the knowledge that he was the first still refused to register in their entirety. But they were slowly beginning to.

He was humbled.

He was hungry.

Hungry for the feel of her, the taste, the scent and the intoxicating wonder of her. He felt as if he were going to die if he couldn't feast on what he craved.

Heart hammering, his lips sealed to hers, Cade pushed the dress down farther along her arms. The tight sleeves released their hold, finally freeing her hands. The material slid fluidly from her hips, falling to the floor like a deep sigh.

McKayla was nude from the waist up.

Even though he knew she would be, verifying it for himself created sudden, intense waves of heat and passion within him. Moaning her name, Cade gathered her to him, losing himself in the silky feel of her skin, the sweet taste of her mouth, the slight whiff of perfume in her hair.

Passion consumed him, leaving no corner untouched. The more he took, the more he wanted.

The more he needed her.

With each kiss, each caress, each inch she surrendered to him, Mac became that much more empowered. Feeding on his needs, and hers, as if it was actual sustenance. The more she gave, the more she had, until she felt as if the surging sensations within her body would actually cause her to burst.

The safe feeling he'd given her gave way to desire of such huge proportions, she was nearly overwhelmed by it. With no thought to consequences, she allowed herself to be swept away, and by the very act, discovered new territories within herself she'd never suspected existed.

He made her aware of everything. The texture of the floor, the height of the walls, the warmth of the light from the lamp. Everything was better, more intense because of him.

She wanted to remain in this place he'd created for her forever. And yet, she rushed to take each new joy, each new explosion within her body, savoring it as if it would be her last.

Eagerly, she tore his clothing from him, not even aware that she was behaving like some untamed force of nature, not yet civilized by society. Not yet imprisoned by its rules. She bore no resemblance to Dr. McKayla Dellaventura. And she didn't care.

They made love on the floor, on the table, on the bed. It was as if speed and direction, time and space, all had melded into a giant canvas. Lovemaking was the brush that allowed them to paint, to leave their mark not only on the weave of the fabric stretched across the wooden boards, but on each other.

Explosion after lush explosion took her body, leaving her damp, perspiring, desperate for rest. Desperate for more. His hands, his tongue, his very breath on the most intimate parts of her, all contributed to the sensations. All could raise her to a fever pitch that bordered on frenzy.

Clutching at him with fingers that had become all but lax, she drew him up to her, arching her hips invitingly. Silently begging for the union he could no longer deny either one of them.

The groan that escaped as he slid into her was a melding of both their voices. Both their desires. Sheathed within her welcoming body, Cade wove his fingers through hers, holding them high over her head, and slowly initiated the dance that took them, partnered, to a summit meant for only two.

She couldn't catch her breath. Her mind was spinning. The force of the climax left her dazed, disoriented and delusional.

Because she felt she was in love with him.

Cade literally left her gasping for air as she sank down to earth again, acutely aware of the brush of his body balanced over hers, hardly noting the weight that went along with it. She didn't want to move. Didn't want him to move. Ever.

In a dreamy stupor, she left her arms encircled around his back, content to remain that way indefinitely. Perhaps longer.

From some dark, mysterious place, she discovered a sliver of energy that enabled her to quip, "Well, that took care of the first hour. What do we do for the other eleven?''

Cade had just had her. And wanted her all over again. The realization left him utterly stunned. He almost felt like a spectator in his own life.

With laughter in his eyes, he raised himself up on his elbows and looked at her. Damp hair was plastered to her forehead. He felt his body quickening at the very sight of her. Was this normal? Or was he in the grips of some kind of devilish spell?

His mouth curved as he pressed a kiss to her neck. ''Does the word *encore* mean anything to you?''

If anyone had asked, Mac would have sworn that used dust rags had more available energy than she had at this moment. And yet, something was beginning to sweetly stir at the feel of his lips along her skin.

''In this case, it would be coupled with the word *bravo*. But I believe that part's up to you.''

''To us,'' he corrected her, his voice low, his breath rippling along her skin. ''To us.''

Cade pulled up the hand brake on the car but remained where he was. They were parked at the curb of a street within a quiet, residential neighborhood. Tall, imported trees with ponderous foliage lined both sides of the street. Except for the song of a bird or two, there was no noise. It was hardly the place one would have thought babies were being sold to the wealthiest couples.

Taylor had called them less than an hour ago, giving them directions to where they would be allowed to meet the child they had ''selected.'' Heather. Supposedly Heather's mother was to be there, waiting for payment. A bogus check for twenty-five thousand dollars was in Mac's purse. It was, Taylor had specified, to be made out to his firm.

After Taylor's call, Cade and Mac had gotten into the car immediately, driving fast, afraid that some last-minute change would rob them of their dearly sought goals.

Mac hadn't said five words since they'd gotten the call. She sat in the passenger seat, her shoulders as rigid as a model soldier's. Cade placed a hand over hers. "Nervous?"

She had been at first, but she was miles past that feeling now.

His question galvanized her. "I'm too angry to be nervous," she told him as she opened the car door.

Mac looked at Cade. "All I want to do right now is to see some action."

Cade didn't doubt it. Didn't doubt, either, that her anger, once aroused, could go a long way in equalizing her to someone bigger in size. The woman was a veritable wildcat when she made love; furious, she was probably a force of nature to be reckoned with.

He suppressed the smile the image of a pumped-up McKayla rendered. He closed the door on his side. "Remind me never to get you angry at me."

"Deal."

Mac's eyes never left the small, one-story house Taylor had sent them to. The house, he had told them, belonged to a go-between. A woman who took in pregnant girls down on their luck. A woman who undoubtedly lulled unsuspecting girls into trusting her before she persuaded them to sign their babies away.

Or, in this case, aided and abetted the kidnapping of children for monetary gain.

Mac wanted to rip her heart out and stomp on it.

A great many revelations had occurred during the short space of time she'd been involved in regaining Heather. She'd never known she was capable of such a wide spectrum of emotions, good and bad.

Someone was going to have to impersonate Heather's mother, Mac thought as they came up the short walk to the front door. Would it be Shirley Lambert or someone else in the organization? She couldn't help wondering how many so-called actors and actresses were involved in this ugly business. Would they get them all? Or would some escape, like a virus that couldn't be fully contained, and allowed to spread in some other place? God, she hoped not.

Out of the corner of her eye, Mac noticed Cade looking around. He was edgy. She'd come too far not to trust his instincts. "What's the matter?"

It could be nothing, but Cade didn't think so. "I don't see Taylor's car, do you?" Thorough to the last detail, they had gotten that kind of information through Redhawk.

Mac's eyes swept over both sides of the street. He was right. "No. Maybe he parked in their garage." It didn't seem likely. The garage door was closed.

"Maybe." It was apparent from his tone that he didn't think so, either.

They walked up the five steps to the front door and rang the bell. When there was no answer, Cade rang again. Still nothing.

Exchanging looks, Mac impatiently indicated the door. Of like mind, Cade tried the knob. To his surprise, it gave. The door wasn't locked. But as Mac took a step forward to enter, he held his hand up, blocking her. He didn't like this. He didn't know why and wasn't able to explain it to himself, much less to Mac, but he just didn't like it. Something wasn't right.

Motioning Mac behind him, knowing she wouldn't remain outside, Cade slowly walked in, a man taking the first step across a minefield.

The image of the handgun with its long, disfiguring silencer registered in the split second before Cade threw himself to the floor, simultaneously pulling Mac down with him. The sickening sound of bullets, muted in their journey, registered as they flew over their heads. In a half crouch, Cade scrambled for cover behind a flowered, overstuffed sofa with Mac directly in his shadow.

Mac didn't have time to think, just react. The air still partially knocked out of her by the fall, she dove for the protection the sofa afforded, pressing herself against it.

She jerked her head up in time to see a gun materialize in Cade's hand. How long had he had that with him? The thought ricocheted through her head, mimicking the beat of the weapon as Cade returned fire. The sound exploded as she watched the bullet take down the man she recognized as the private detective who had been tailing them.

This is all wrong.

The uneasy thought beat an edgy tattoo in her breast. She felt numb and stunned all at the same time as she tried to make sense out of what had just happened.

They'd been set up.

Beside her, Cade was on his feet again.

He wanted the hired thug masquerading as a private investigator to have no opportunity to get a second drop on them. Blood was flowing from the man's wound, seeping in between his fingers as he pressed his hand to his shoulder. Luck only held for so long before it shredded. He kept his gun trained on the man.

"McKayla, find something to tie him up with," Cade ordered.

There was nothing in the immediate area that seemed strong enough to use. Mac hurried into the garage. Tossing cans and boxes around that were in her way, she finally found a length of hemp. The coarse rope bit into her flesh as she yanked it up from beneath some boards.

Flying back into the house, she quickly tied the P.I.'s hands behind his back, ignoring the violent volley of curses.

"Where's Heather?" she demanded.

Loathing flared in the brown eyes. "Who the hell is Heather?"

Cade spun the man around so that he faced him squarely. "The little girl Taylor thought we wanted to adopt."

The detective warily eyed the weapon that was close to his temple. "I don't know anything about any little girl." Sweat began to ooze along his forehead. "Hey, look, I'm bleeding all over the place here. This is all just a big mistake."

"Yeah, and you made it." The need for discretion had passed. It was obvious that Taylor and Lambert

were on to them. They had to act fast now. Cade
cocked the trigger. "Where is he holding the kids?"

"Beats me."

"Don't think I won't," Cade growled.

The temptation to vent his frustration was great, but
he managed to contain himself. Shoving the man
ahead of him, he pushed him to the open door.

"Shall I call 911, Mr. Taylor?" his secretary asked,
remaining where she'd been pushed by the young
woman who was now storming into his office.

The slim microphone he was dictating into slid
from his fingers as if they had suddenly become bone-
less. The first thought that telegraphed itself through
his mind was that he'd thought these two had been
taken care of.

Mac answered for Taylor. "Yes, why don't you do
that?" She shifted her eyes to the lawyer, making no
effort to suppress the loathing she felt. "Call 911. Ask
for Lieutenant Graham Redhawk while you're at it.
I'm sure he and Mr. Taylor would find a great deal
to talk about, wouldn't you, Taylor?"

Taylor's eyes hardened. With a flick of his wrist,
he waved his secretary away. "Never mind, Eugenia.
I can handle this."

"I wouldn't bet on it this time." Cade's voice was
low and all the more dangerous for its steely sound.
He saw the lawyer wince involuntarily as he approached. "What happened? Why weren't you at the
house?"

Taylor's eyes darted toward the doorway.
"Where's Fowler?"

Cade raised a brow, looking at Taylor with mild

interest. "You mean the man you sent to kill us? Right now, he's at the police precinct." Cade leaned in, bringing his face close to Taylor's so that the man heard every syllable, every nail being hammered into his coffin. "If you concentrate really hard, you can feel him rolling over on you right about now."

A slight edge of panic began to prick at Taylor. He was to have remained above all this, above the dirty details and the consequences. "I don't know what you're talking about."

His patience dangerously limited, Cade yanked Taylor up by his shirt, literally pulling him out of his chair. "Then try concentrating a little harder. I'm talking about kids, Taylor. Innocent little kids snatched from their families and used in the dirty little business you and Lambert are running."

"I don't know—"

Cade's hold tightened, cutting Taylor's air supply by half. "You deny it again, and I'm going to rip your tongue out, tie it in a knot and make you swallow it."

"You're a madman." Gasping for air, Taylor shifted furtive eyes toward the woman, but her expression gave him no more to hope for than her partner's did. He thought of shouting for help, but knew that was futile even before he attempted it.

"Yes, I am, mad as hell." Cade struggled with the very real urge to snuff Taylor's insignificant life out. The satisfaction would have been enormous, and there would've been no chance of Taylor getting off because of some sleight of hand executed by a good lawyer. "You have my son and her niece, and if you want to get out of this room alive, by God you're going to tell us where they are.''

''But I don't know—'' Fear had replaced bravado. Survival was all that mattered. Taylor whimpered as he felt the powerful hand closing over his throat, squeezing the air away. In another moment, there would be none left. ''No, please,'' he rasped, frantically begging for his life. ''I don't know who they are.''

Mac placed her hand on Cade's shoulder, afraid that he was going to kill the man with his bare hands. Taylor and Lambert had tainted their lives enough. There was nothing to be gained by squashing a roach like Taylor. Cade wasn't the kind of man who would derive satisfaction out of knowing he had killed anyone, even someone like Taylor.

''Cade, let him go.'' She shook his shoulder, trying to bring him around. ''I know what you're going through, but he's not going to be any use to us dead.'' He wasn't releasing him. Her voice took on a sharp edge. She had to get through to him, had to make him stop. He couldn't ruin his life because of Taylor. ''And you can't be reunited with your son if you're in jail for murder.'' The look of gratitude that came into Taylor's eyes turned her stomach. ''Even if it is justified.''

With an oath borne of all the tortured years of fruitless searching, Cade cursed the emptiness that should have been Taylor's soul and released him, throwing him back into his chair.

''Talk,'' he demanded.

Tears rolled down the weathered face. ''I don't know which one she is.'' An unearthly sound escaped his dry lips as Cade took a step toward him. His hands, which he raised before him to ward Cade off, were trembling. "Please," he pleaded with Mac. "I want to see the D.A. I'll make a deal—"

More time lost. Cade couldn't stand for it. Wouldn't stand for it. He jerked Taylor up to his feet again. "The deal is you get to rot in hell, starting five minutes from now, if you don't tell me what I want to know."

Cowering, Taylor bobbed his head. "All right. I'll tell you where they're being kept. I have coded records on all the adoptions." His hand jerked spasmodically as he pointed to his computer. "Just please, please don't kill me."

"Talk," Cade ordered. "And then we'll see if you live."

Mac had absolutely no reason to doubt that he meant it. It was over, she thought, relief flooding her. She'd have Heather back before nightfall.

If there was a tinge of something else lurking in the background, the tiniest shadow of regret because something else would be over as well, she pretended not to notice, because regret would be incredibly selfish of her and she had never been a selfish woman.

Chapter 15

There was a darkness in the room that the sunlight couldn't seem to eradicate.

The little boy looked at him with wide, frightened eyes. He sat on the recliner, trying to make himself as small as possible, trying to disappear into the soft, black leather.

It broke Cade's heart to see him like this. The child he'd been looking so hard for all these long years didn't know him. Worse, was afraid of him.

Wanting to rush in and sweep Darin into his arms, Cade forced himself to take small, slow steps toward the boy instead. He dropped to his knees beside the recliner. Darin pressed his body even farther into the cushions. Anger fought with joy.

"What did they do to you, Darin?"

Confusion joined fear. Darin shook his dark head. "Not Darin, can't be Darin. Jeremy now. My name's Jeremy."

Mac pressed her lips together, sympathy over-whelming her. Her arms filled with her niece, Mac was reluctant to let her go, even for a moment. There'd been recognition in Heather's eyes when she'd entered the nursery in another section of the house where the little girl was being kept. It would have been brutal if she'd had to face the fear that Cade saw now.

She laid a comforting hand on his shoulder. "He's afraid of you."

"Don't you think I know that?" Cade muttered, then flushed. Anguish hummed in every syllable. "I'm sorry."

There was no need to apologize. She understood. They needed a bridge, something to stir a distant, not quite forgotten memory. "Maybe if you talk to him about what you used to do together..."

His mind suddenly a blank, Cade struggled to sum-mon bits and pieces of their lives before Darin had been torn away from him. What would Darin have remembered? Still crouching down to the boy's level, Cade was oblivious to the fact that Mac and Redhawk were looking on. The room could have been filled with people, it would have made no difference. All there was for him was Darin. The son who wasn't back yet.

"Do you remember watching cartoons with me on Saturday mornings, Darin?"

The dark eyes stared straight ahead, not looking at him. "Jeremy."

Frustration flared. He clamped it down.

"Jeremy," Cade repeated, though the very name tasted bitter to his tongue. He thought harder. "Do you remember Spotty the dog?'' The cartoon creation had been his son's favorite character. He still had the tapes that Darin had loved to watch over and over. ''I got you a stuffed Spotty and you carried it around everywhere.'' Cade's voice grew in momentum as he desperately tried to break through the invisible barriers that kept him from his son. ''When you lost it, I drove around for hours trying to find it for you. It turned out to be in our garage all the time.''

There was no change in expression, no acknowledgment. Nothing. He wasn't getting through to Darin. It ripped Cade's soul to be here with his child, after all this time, and not find him within the boy who sat here now, stoically ignoring him. What had they done to his son?

Mac exchanged looks with Redhawk. The latter shook his head, as stymied as he was saddened to witness this. ''Try a favorite story,'' Mac whispered to Cade.

He blew out a breath. ''He didn't have one. He liked everything I read to him.''

Mac shifted her niece's weight slightly, moving her farther up on her hip. She tried to think of the way she played with Heather.

''A favorite song?'' she guessed. ''Did he have a favorite song? Did you sing to him?''

Cade began to say no, and then he remembered. ''Yeah, there was one. 'Me and My Shadow.''' Excitement built on the shaky foundation of unrooted hope. ''He was like my little shadow, and one day the song just popped into my head. We sang it all the time.''

She'd seen a flicker of something in the boy's eyes

when Cade had mentioned the old song. "Try it," she urged. Mentally, Mac crossed her fingers. "Try singing it to him."

There seemed to be no breath left in his lungs. The words were hardly audible, pushing their way up a throat that felt swollen and chafed, thick with tears that he was repressing. Defeat crept in. Cade stopped at the third chorus. There was nothing in Darin's face to show that the boy even vaguely remembered.

Turning away, Cade looked at Mac and Redhawk. "I guess it's going to take longer than I—"

Jeremy's small, solemn voice broke in as he sang a line from the song, picking up the words where Cade had left off.

For a split second, Cade froze. And then the ice cracked from around his heart.

"You remember!" Spinning around, he scooped the boy up into his arms. Tears instantly formed in the corners of his eyes and streamed down his cheeks. It was going to be all right. His son had returned to him. "You remember."

He buried his face in the boy's neck as he held him to him, breathing in the sweet scent of Darin's skin.

Mac didn't even bother trying not to cry.

Darin's initial reaction was to squirm and try to get away, but the impulse seemed to leave quickly and his body relaxed against his father's. He looked confused, but the fear, the distrust, had miraculously melted away. He closed his arms around his father's neck and held on tightly.

"Why are you crying, Daddy?"

Daddy. It was by far the sweetest word he'd ever

heard. Cade raised his head and looked at the boy, kissing his face. "Because I'm happy."

The boy turned uncomprehending eyes toward Mac.

Unable to resist, she ruffled the dark hair, her own heart bursting. "When you grow up, you'll understand," she promised. "Trust me."

He looked as if he were trying to place her in the new scheme of things. "Are you Mommy?" There was pure innocence in the question.

"No, I'm not." But even as she said it, Mac suddenly realized that she wanted to be. Wanted to be his mommy and Cade's wife. Wanted this kind of warmth as her own. Maybe she wanted it, she thought, because it, this man, and his life, felt so far beyond her reach and there was a safety in pretending.

Or maybe she was finally ready to take the chance on loving someone.

For the life of her, she wasn't sure.

"Hey, Lieutenant." One of the uniformed officers stuck his head in. "We need you for a second."

Moved by what he'd just witnessed, Gray called back, "I'll be there in a minute," and approached Cade. Thinking of his own son, he ran his hand along the boy's hair. "A lot of people are going to be very grateful to you two. We found over a hundred files so far. A hundred kids adopted under suspicious circumstances. As near as we can figure it out right now, the organization had several photo studios in California, Arizona, and Nevada. Unsuspecting parents would bring their newborns and toddlers in for photographs, and the studios showed the shots to Lambert and his partner who made their pick and the 'leg man' would go into action. The addresses and pertinent information were all on file at the studios. As close to catching fish in a barrel as you are going to come. It's going to take a lot of people working around the clock to unscramble this, but in the end, there are going to be a great many relieved families.'' He looked at both of them. ''Anything either of you need?''

There was only one thing that he wanted now. ''How about an escort to the airport?'' Cade suggested. He glanced at Mac for confirmation. She nodded. ''I think we'd all like to go home.''

It was the least he could do for them, Redhawk thought. ''You got it.''

Word of the black-market baby ring breakup had preceded them.

When their plane landed at John Wayne Airport, the terminal was crowded to overflowing with the news media. Cameras, microphones and a sea of questions swirled around Cade and Mac as they tried to make their way from the gate to the escalator that would take them to the ground floor and freedom.

Mac hugged a whimpering Heather to her. The child was clearly frightened. Even Darin was clinging tightly to Cade. Cade tried to shield them all as best he could, walking ahead of Mac and Heather.

''How the hell did they manage to find out so soon?'' he shouted to her above the noise. Aware of the high profile this case would receive, he still hadn't thought he'd have to face the media frenzy so soon. All he wanted was some time alone with his son.

''Someone in my family must have told someone.''

Mac had called her mother on the cell phone the first opportunity she had, even before they boarded the plane. She wanted to set everyone's mind at ease, especially Moira's. Her parents were closemouthed and she doubted they'd told anyone beyond the immediate family, but her brothers were a different story. Danny and Randy thought happiness was something to be shared.

Mac had made another call as well, but she was willing to bet that no one on that end was the source of this media "leak." It was expressly for this reason that she'd told her family not to come. That she would bring Heather to them at home. Moira, though released from the hospital, was still in no condition to encounter this kind of media circus.

He laughed shortly. Every second, there seemed to be more people joining the throng. "Looks that way."

And then he saw a familiar face. A police detective he'd met through Sam. The latter had gone through the police academy with Ben Underwood. Behind Ben, Cade could make out Sam and Rusty coming toward them. Before he knew it, they had formed a human ring around them. He'd never been so glad to see them as he was at this moment.

Megan brushed a quick kiss to his cheek. "We thought we'd run interference for you. Welcome home, Dad." She beamed at the boy in Cade's arms. "You are the most welcome sight, Darin Townsend." Remembering, she suddenly produced a battered stuffed animal out of her bag and gave it to Cade's son.

Recognition and glee were instantaneous. Darin

squealed as he immediately hugged the toy to him. "Spotty."

Cade was speechless. And utterly grateful. "What made you—"

Megan held up her hands. "Wasn't my idea. Mac called me. She had a hunch you still had this old thing lying around somewhere. She suggested I round it up and bring it to the airport." Megan grinned as she watched Darin. "Looks like she was right."

So it had been Mac who had summoned them. And Mac who, even in the middle of her own reunion, had thought to help him bond with his son. Not knowing what to say, Cade looked at her over his shoulder and mouthed "Thanks." Her smile told him that she understood.

And then, the news media closed ranks around them, tightening the circle despite the human wall there to protect them.

"C'mon, Cade, give us a few words—" a newscaster directly in front of him coaxed.

They'd been good to him, the media, he thought. As much as he wanted just to go home with his son, Cade knew he owed these people something. They had put his story on page one, following it up periodically. And through his story, they had brought people into his life whom he had been able to help. And brought one person who had inadvertently helped him by leading him to his son. He couldn't turn his back on them now.

Cade paused and looked at them, not seeing a single face clearly. There was too much going on inside of him to focus or see clearly. That would come later, when emotions settled down to a subdued roar.

He grinned at the newscaster directly in front of him and bent over his microphone. "I'll give you a few words. It looks like ChildFinders, Inc., finally has that perfect record now."

Everyone loved a happy ending, and the people of the media were no different. They enjoyed being the bearer of good news as well as the intriguing, the mystifying and the bad. Questions continued flying at Cade, coming from all directions. Holding his son to him, smiling for the cameras, he fielded the ones he could make out to the best of his ability.

As she listened to Cade, Mac suddenly felt a hand on her arm. Turning quickly, she saw Megan at her elbow.

"I've got my car parked pretty close to the terminal," Megan whispered into her ear. "Your family's waiting at the office for you. C'mon," she urged. "Let's get you out of here. This might take a while." She nodded toward Cade.

Mac wanted to remain. To listen to Cade talk. To watch the light in his eyes and on his face. This was his moment and it had been deservedly earned. The man had been to hell and back and had not only survived, but beaten devastating odds.

Somewhere in her heart she also knew this would be the last time they'd be this close to each other.

She wanted to stay.

But there was responsibility beckoning to her. There was still that last leg of the journey to make before she had fulfilled her promise. She'd promised to place Heather into Moira's arms.

Her family was waiting.

Grateful for Megan's help, Mac nodded at her. "Thanks," she murmured.

Catching his eye, Megan signaled to her brother that she was leaving with Mac and Heather. Rusty gave her the high sign as he kept close to Cade, his large frame holding back the crowd on one side.

Looking over her shoulder as she followed Megan from the floor, Mac mouthed "Goodbye" to Cade. She knew he didn't see her, certainly didn't hear her, but then, she hadn't expected him to.

It was enough that she had said it. If her heart ached a little as she left, she was determined to ignore it.

It was driving her crazy.

It had been two whole weeks now, and Mac still couldn't get rid of the restlessness. You would have thought that once she'd brought Heather home, once the dust had all settled and people stopped coming around to talk about the kidnapping and the rescue and Cade, life would get back to normal.

It didn't.

The restlessness that had accompanied her on this odyssey not only to recover Heather, but also into self-awareness as well, was still with her. Shadowing her every move.

To make things worse, bits and pieces of "Me and My Shadow" insisted on playing, over and over again, in her head. Haunting her. Giving her no peace.

He didn't call. She wanted to, but didn't. It wasn't her move to make. Forceful though she was, she wasn't about to be told that what they'd had was "just one of those things.'' One old song ricocheting in her mind was more than enough.

She couldn't find a place for herself. Couldn't go on with her life because, like scratchy branches, the events of the recent past kept snaring her. Pulling at her. Holding her back. Having every parent who brought their child into her office ask her for details didn't help, either. It certainly didn't allow her to put any of it behind her no matter how much she tried.

As soon as she'd returned to her own home, Mac had written the agency a check for the agreed-upon amount, plus a large bonus as a donation. She would have done the latter even if her father and brothers hadn't given her the money. Cade, she knew, was going to keep the agency going. He'd told her so on the plane trip back. There was a need for a firm like his, one that specifically concentrated on finding lost and abducted children and reuniting them with their families.

She'd read a confirmation of the same in the paper just the other day. The newspaper and news programs were the only way she was getting her information about Cade these days.

But then, she hadn't really expected him to call once this was over. They'd had a unique, fleeting relationship. They'd been a team on the road. A good team. But the playing season was over, and it was time to hang up the uniform. And the memories.

Even if she didn't believe it, she thought, slipping her lab coat on, Cade obviously did. Otherwise, he would have tried to call her. God knew she'd checked her answering machine and the caller I.D. listings often enough.

His number never appeared. His voice was never there.

He wanted to put everything behind him, her included. She couldn't fault him.

The hell she couldn't.

Frustrated, Mac pushed the movable arm on the exam chair so hard, it groaned.

But faulting him or not, it didn't make a difference. Cade wasn't in her life by choice, and she wasn't about to make a monumental fool out of herself and show up on his doorstep no matter how much she ached to. His life was obviously full without her.

And hers felt oddly empty, no matter how hard she worked, how busy she kept.

Served her right for letting herself care. She'd known what a risk that would be. And now she was experiencing it all firsthand. She was just going to have to work through this until it faded.

And how long was that going to take?

She'd been working nonstop since the day after she returned. When there was a lull in her own patient load, she took on some of her father's and brother's. Mac's intent was to keep at it until she dropped. And couldn't think.

Because they sensed something was wrong, that she needed to keep up this frenzied pace until she worked something out of her system, her father and Danny sent patients her way. And hoped for the best.

It wasn't working. Instead of getting better, it was becoming worse. Moreover, the pace was catching up to her. Not to where she was liable to make errors in judgment, but like a soldier stationed at the front lines, she was beginning to feel the effects of battle fatigue.

And she wasn't even enlisted in the war anymore.

Mac tried to think and remember what day it was. Tuesday? Thursday? They were all beginning to run together for her. She hated this feeling. Hated this hurt. When was it going to stop?

She rubbed the bridge of her nose, wishing she could rub away the headache that persisted in lingering there. The headache was well into its second week, showing no signs of retreat. It figured.

Mac debated taking two more aspirins, but her consumption of late already rivaled that of the entire population of Los Angeles. Taking more wouldn't help. Nothing was going to help, except for time.

Maybe.

Her dental assistant, Angie, popped her head in the small room. "Heads up, Dr. Mac, you've got a new patient coming your way."

Another child to win over, Mac thought with resignation. Initial trips to the dentist were not viewed in the same light as first trips to Disneyland. Normally, she thought of this as a challenge. But she didn't really feel up to challenges anymore.

Still, she couldn't very well send the child to her father, who was the only other dentist in this morning. Her father had an intimidating quality about him that did little to set children's minds at ease.

With a nod, she took out a new box of plastic gloves and placed it on the counter. "Send her on in."

"It's a he," Angie corrected her, handing her the brand-new folder.

"Okay, send him on in." Wearily, she turned the folder around to read the name that was typed on the side. She read it once, then blinked and read it again. It was too much of a stretch of the imagination to think this was just a coincidence. Mac raised her eyes to her assistant. "Angie, is this someone's idea of a joke?"

Angie didn't answer. The tall, dark-haired man behind her did.

"No, we're very serious about our teeth, aren't we, Darin?" he asked the small boy whose hand he was holding.

Darin nodded, trying to look solemn. The next moment, he launched himself at Mac. Achieving target, he wound his arms around her somewhere in the vicinity of her hips as he buried his face against her hip bone. An open, happy child by nature, he'd clearly made great strides in the last two weeks. Even during the flight back from Phoenix, he'd begun to take a shine to Mac.

He looked up at her, a lopsided smile on his lips. "Hi, Mac. Is it going to hurt?"

Her hand on Darin's silky hair, she looked at the boy's father. Why didn't he look the way she felt? No one had a right to look that good, she thought. "He's my new patient?"

For two weeks, Cade had tried to strip his mind of her. He'd tried to harness his emotions and go back to life the way it once had been. But the small niche no longer worked. He had his son back, and a purpose to his life. But he needed more. He needed her.

Cade's eyes held hers as he wondered where to

begin. How to tell her what he was feeling. "You're a pediatric dentist, aren't you?"

"Yes."

Cade gestured toward his son, who was still clinging to her. The two looked as if they belonged together. It just confirmed what he'd been feeling all along. "And he's pediatric-size."

"So he is." She looked down at the boy. "No, Darin, it's not going to hurt. Not even a little bit. I promise."

Concentrating on making Darin comfortable and not on what his presence here actually meant, she picked him up and placed him in the examination chair. It took her a moment to remember what to do next. She reached for the Polaroid camera on the far end of the counter. A gift from Moira when she graduated from dental school.

She aimed the camera at Darin. "Smile." It was a needless instruction. The boy was grinning ear to ear. She snapped twice.

A moment later, the camera spit out first one photograph, then another at its heels. She presented the first one to Cade. "A photograph to take home to remind you of his first examination."

Cade noticed that she kept the second one herself. It was a nice touch, he thought. Darin had his hand out, and he gave him the photograph. Like a child watching a magic act, Darin stared intently at the photograph as his image began to materialize right before his eyes. He was properly impressed.

"I don't think I'll need a photograph to remind me," Cade told Mac. "But I wouldn't mind taking the dentist home with me."

If Mac didn't know that it was medically impossible, she would have said her heart stopped beating. Collecting herself, she pointed toward the overhead TV set. There was a children's video running.

"Why don't you watch that for a few minutes, Darin? I'd like a word with your father."

Cade followed her to just outside the door. "That has an ominous sound to it."

She whirled on her heel, her eyes flashing. It took effort to keep her voice low when her temper was flaring so high. "You bet it does. You don't even pick up a phone in two weeks to ask if I'm alive and now you stroll in here like nothing happened—"

"A great deal happened," he interjected quietly, stopping her before she could get up a full head of steam. "That was just the trouble. I had to sort it all out." The words were still not coming together the way he would have liked. He just had to trust that she would understand. "When my wife died, I swore to myself that I'd never love anyone again. It wasn't a hard promise to keep because something died inside of me along with her." His eyes held hers and he remembered what it was like, making love with her. And wanting to do it over and over again. To get lost in her strength and her vulnerability. "At least I thought it did, until you walked into my office and my life. And into parts of me I could have sworn were gone for good."

"And that's why you didn't call?"

He knew it sounded strange, but it was true. "Yes, that's why I didn't call. Because I tried to tell myself I was reacting to the situation, to the moment. And then, to the elation of finding Darin. With all that going on, it's easy to lose your perspective. But it wasn't my perspective I lost." Cade wanted to touch her, to hold her. He appeased himself by looking into her eyes. "It was my heart." Resistance proved futile. He cupped his hand to her cheek, caressing her softly. "Like it or not, I'm in love with you, McKayla."

There were a hundred things Mac had called him in her mind. If her life depended on it, she couldn't remember a single one.

"I like it," she said softly.

Relieved, Cade took her into his arms. "Good, then this next part might just work out."

"What next part?"

He could make her happy, he knew he could. And he wanted to spend the rest of his life doing it if she let him. "Marry me."

Mac had to be hearing things. But one look at his face told her that she wasn't. He'd just proposed. "Just like that?"

"No, not just like that. First we have to get a license, blood tests—"

"Wait, wait—" She stopped him before he could go on. This wasn't a joke or a prank, she realized. And if it was a dream, then she was in big trouble. "Are you being serious?"

The smile on his face softened until it was a shade away from solemn. He feathered his fingers through her hair. God, but he had missed her. Missed her so much that it ached even now, even though he was holding her. "Never more serious in my life."

Mac felt as if she'd just had the wind knocked out of her. "But—so fast?"

"A minute ago, you were accusing me of being too

slow because I hadn't called. You can't have it both ways, McKayla."

She could feel her pulse jumping up and down her entire body. It was a wonder she wasn't vibrating, she thought. "Which way can I have it?"

He brought his lips to hers, but only touched them lightly. "Hopefully, with me."

"What's my other choice?" When he looked at her in worried surprise, she laughed, then kissed him hard on the mouth. "Gotcha! Yes, I'll marry you." She saw the question in his eyes. "And yes, I love you," she added more softly.

After so long, things were finally arranging themselves in his life. It was almost hard to believe. "Then we're on the same page?"

On her toes, she wound her arms around his neck. She was aware that Angie was peeking out of one of the cubicles, watching, but she didn't care. Everyone would know soon enough. "On the same page, in the same book, on the same shelf."

Cade grinned, tightening his hold on her. In the background, he heard Darin giggling over something he was watching. It was an incredibly heartwarming sound. "Does this mean Darin gets free dental care?"

"Whenever I'm not too busy with his dad."

"Oh. Then I guess for the first hundred years, we'd better get him another dentist."

She looked at him in mock disappointment. "Just the first hundred?"

"After that, we'll see."

"Deal," she murmured just before he pressed his lips to hers.

Epilogue

"Two hands, Darin. Hold on to the reins with two hands."

Craning his neck, Cade watched his son disappear from view as the merry-go-round whirled gaily, the horses moving in time to a popular children's tune. Though he knew he shouldn't, he held his breath until Darin reappeared on the other side, this time dutifully holding on to the reins of the cream-colored horse with both hands.

He supposed he could have postponed this, waited a little longer. But it had already been a year, and he'd always believed in facing your own demons. Returning to the amusement park where Darin had been kidnapped to celebrate his birthday would be therapeutic for both of them. He just had to remember to relax.

Darin was doing a far better job of that than he was, Cade thought, watching him.

"Aren't you being just a wee-bit overprotective?" Mac threaded her arms around his.

These days, that wasn't the easiest thing to do. Not when her stomach with its temporary tenant was always getting in the way.

Cade laughed softly to himself. He didn't want to hold Darin back. He would have hated having his parents hover over him at that age. "You're right. I've got to work on letting him be six. I mean seven."

Mac nodded her agreement, a bemused smile playing on her lips. "And then eight, and then nine…"

"Hey, don't rush me." Cade held up a warning hand, as if to ward off time. As if it were that easy. "One step at a time."

She'd forgotten what it felt like to find a comfortable position, Mac thought, shifting beside Cade. She covered her abdomen protectively as she pretended to eye him. "Are you going to be this way with Bernice or Horatio when they're born?"

Cade winced at the names she flung out arbitrarily. She'd been doing this for the last nine months, trying to find one of each she liked fitting her tongue around. Was it him or had the names gotten more eccentric in the last couple of weeks?

"I am if you're going to call them that. Otherwise, they'll have the tar beaten out of them by the neighborhood bullies." He looked at her. "You're not really serious, are you?"

"About you and Darin, yes." The somber expression gave way to the slightest grin. "About the names…I can be bribed."

One arm around her shoulders, he hugged her to him. "With?"

Mac paused, considering. "I'll have to think about it." Her eyes danced as she looked up at him. She couldn't remember when she had been happier, even if she couldn't see her feet anymore. "Just your luck, you had to marry a larcenous woman."

"Yeah." Impulsively, he kissed her temple. "Just my luck." All good since the day she walked into his office, exactly one year ago today.

The carousel had stopped a minute earlier, and now Darin came flying over to them. "Did you see? Did you see me, Daddy?"

In the last year, the boy had shot up a couple of inches and filled out a little. He no longer looked gaunt or frightened. There were no leftover ill-effects from the ordeal he had gone through. Cade thought of himself as one of the lucky ones.

He went to embrace the boy, then abruptly held himself in check. Darin didn't think "big boys" hugged in public. So he settled on ruffling the boy's hair. "Never took my eyes off you, champ."

Taking a step backwards, Darin bumped into Mac's stomach. She felt the baby kick hard enough to send a football over the goal post.

"Ow." Swinging around, Darin stared at Mac's stomach. He rubbed his ribs. "I think Humphrey just kicked me."

"Humphrey?" Cade echoed incredulously, looking from his son to his wife. "You've got him doing it, too?"

Mac raised her chin proudly, slipping her arm around Darin's slim shoulders. He'd taken to calling her mom. It pleased her a great deal. "Strength in numbers."

Darin raised his eyes to her. "Does this mean the baby wants to get out?"

She nodded. "Pretty soon."

Darin grinned at her answer. His exuberant expression took in both his parents. "This is the best birthday ever."

Throat tightening, Cade came between them and slipped an arm around his wife and one around his son, drawing them both closer to him. "You know, I was just thinking the same thing myself."

* * * * *

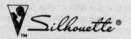

If you enjoyed what you just read,
then we've got an offer you can't resist!

Take 2 bestselling love stories FREE!
Plus get a FREE surprise gift!

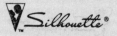

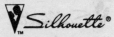

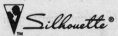

COMING NEXT MONTH